Praise

"Incisive, amusing, thought-provoking. These stories are unputdownable."

~ Carol Ardman, author, *Tangier Love Story*

"Ray Fortunato's short stories are entertaining, thought provoking and no topic is off limits. Each story is unique, full of humor, quirkiness and insight."

~ Theresa Drescher, author,
The Upside to Everything, Even Breast Cancer

"Raymond Fortunato's stories frequently make you think about why and how you think the things you think, for they depict stereotypical patterns of thought that can lead us mortals astray. Reading them, I have wondered how Socrates had managed to live long enough to write for 'The Twilight Zone.'"

~ Louis Gilbert

"Raymond is a gifted storyteller who plunges readers into the lives of his characters through fast-paced dialogue. His writing never shies away from difficult subjects but always captures the beauty of human relationships. He is at his best when tackling real-life issues that challenge readers to think and explore their own values and feelings. His stories will stay with readers long after the last page is read."

~ Elizabeth Sundstrom

"Each of Ray Fortunato's stories creates a world unto itself. His inventiveness is amazing. And each illuminates the intellectual or emotional world of his characters."

~ Heidi Fiske

"Fortunato's stories were a big hit with myself and the students in my high school Creative Writing class. It was the first time I've ever had a class where all the students spent the whole class period silently reading. It was beautiful."

~ Bruce Marr

"Raymond Fortunato's Nothing's Plenty for Me *offers some strong insight into humanity, exploring what we can do without when given the option while learning to accept others for who they are, and trusting not everyone is really who they seem. There is plenty to appreciate in this play. The scene when the group decides to turn off the heat and electricity and recites poetry on the fly was silly and genuine, showcasing a budding friendship between an unlikely group of friends, and offering hope that change really can happen."*

~ Carissa Cheserek, *Broadway World*

THE
HYPÓKRISIS
MIRROR
AND OTHER STORIES

By Raymond Fortunato

Published Works
Joyful, Sorrowful and Ordinary Mysteries

Theatre
Nothing's Plenty for Me
A dramady about climate change presented by
Xoregos Performing Company at Theatre Row

Music Albums
The Life I Love You Suite
I've Never Seen Your Heart
Anger Stay Away From Me
Hold Me, Squeeze Me, Kiss Me, Tease Me

Dedication

With gratitude to Margaret and Phillip Fortunato.

"A Tiny Pebble" was first published in *The Bangalore Review*, Vol X., Issue 11, April 2023.
"And One" was first published in the *Evening Street Review*, Number 37, Spring 2023.
"Ambitious Alexander" was first published in *Half and One Magazine*, January 18, 2025.
"Elephants Interrupted" was first published in *Half and One Magazine*, January 24, 2024.
"I Should Report You but Officially I Saw Anything" was first published in *Half and One Magazine*, June 1, 2023.
"Mr. Omniscient" was first published in *Every Day Fiction*, December 20, 2024.
"The Great Silence" was first published in *The Red Hyacinth Journal of Writing and Art*, Spring 2024.
"The *Hypókrisis* Mirror" was first published in *The Write Launch*, April 2023.
"The Personal Statement" was first published in *Half and One Magazine*, July 9, 2024.
"What Are You Going to Do with Your Life" was first published in *Half and One Magazine*, October 6, 2023

Published in the United States by Raymond Fortunato, May 5, 2026.

ISBN 979-8-9951908-0-6 *The Hypókrisis Mirror and Other Stories*

Raymond Fortunato
RaymondFortunato.com

Editorial Production by Artea Creative
Cover designed by Robin Locke Monda
Book Interior designed by Daiana Morales
Distributed by IngramSpark

The Library of Congress has catalogued this work as follows:

The Hypókrisis Mirror and Other Stories / Raymond Fortunato. — 1st printing.
979-8-9951908-0-6
Library of Congress Control Number: 2026906802.
1.   Adult—Fiction-Short Stories 2. Fiction_Short Stories 3. Fiction_General

THE HYPÓKRISIS MIRROR

AND OTHER STORIES

RAYMOND FORTUNATO

Contents

THE HYPÓKRISIS MIRROR

To celebrate the hundredth anniversary of the Symington Art Museum's 1913 archeological dig, near the ancient oracle at Delphi in Greece, the museum asked Audrey August, a Classics scholar at Whitson College, to prepare a special exhibit.

Knowing her fellow professor, Rokko Isti's, deep interest in ancient history, Audrey asked him to help. Audrey would re-examine the notes, photographs and stored finds from the dig.

Several weeks after she began, she found a small box, unlabeled except for a sticker that said, "Fragile, Use Caution." There were no notes about what was in this box, so she called Rokko to witness its opening and help if it needed conservation. Inside was a highly corroded, circular bronze mirror, about five inches in diameter on a twelve-inch holder. The mirror was intact, only part of a small piece, about a quarter inch across, was broken off and sat next to the other, larger pieces. On the mirror holder was an inscription in ancient Greek. Audrey read it out in English, "This *hypókrisis* mirror is for the enlightenment of philosophers."

"What a strange inscription," Rokko said. "What do you think it means?"

"I've never read an inscription like it," agreed Audrey, who was beaming, happy at an unexpected discovery. "The Greek word *hypókrisis* meant playing a part on the stage, pretending to be something one is not."

"Playing a part on the stage? Pretending?" asked Rokko. "That's curious."

"Athens had an annual dramatic contest," said Audrey. "Some of the plays were quite philosophical. Maybe this was a prop."

"That might explain it."

"The mirror's an unusual color." Audrey picked it up. Rokko noticed that her hand quivered as she held it. A minute later she looked directly into it.

Rokko could see fear in Audrey's face. "What's the matter?"

Audrey shook her head vigorously, looked at Rokko, blinked twice and put the mirror down. "It's too corroded to see yourself."

Rokko picked up the mirror and tried looking at himself. "There's no image. I feel like I'm looking down from a high balcony and the handrail has disappeared. Very strange."

"We don't need this one. We have a mirror in the original exhibit. Let's pack it back up." They did. Audrey let Rokko take the broken off quarter-inch sliver that lay in the box for conservation and study.

Rokko measured reflected light off the fragment. The light was bent in an erratic manner. He scrapped a tiny bit for a mass spectrometer reading. Besides tin and copper, there were traces of other elements, which Rokko thought might be from one or more rare minerals.

Rokko found an excuse to fly to Greece and spend a few days at the dig site. He found several minerals that he wasn't familiar with. Perhaps a combination of them would make the coating of the mirror. Rocco knew it was illegal to bring stones out of the country, so he crushed them up, mixed them with dirt and rubbed it on all his clothes. No one ever questioned dirty clothes in your luggage.

Rokko spent almost eighteen months before he succeeded at recreating the coating on the mirror. He told no one of his efforts. *Why am I being so secretive*, he wondered. He created three objects that bent the light in the same erratic manner as the original mirror: a mirror, a pair of glasses with no correction and clip-ons to wear over an existing set of glasses.

The next day, Rokko was sitting in his home office. He wondered if he should ask for volunteers to try on the glasses. No. They wouldn't understand. *Maybe if I put them on for a few seconds and ask myself how to test them, I'll get an answer.* He went to the bathroom, put the clip-ons on over his own glasses and looked at himself in the mirror. "I can't believe what I'm seeing," Rokko said out loud. "I don't understand." Ten seconds passed and his breathing became shallow and rapid, dabs of sweat dribbled down his face. He ripped his glasses from his eyes, so violently that they almost broke. The familiar out of focus image of his face returned.

Several minutes passed before Rokko's breath returned to normal. *I wonder if I just had a panic attack. I've never had one before.* When he calmed down, he began to think that he must have been hallucinating when he had these glasses on. *I'm a scientist,* he thought. *This is just an experiment. I have to do it again.*

He went into his study. He stood and looked around the room. On the wall was his most prized possession, the Nobel Prize in Physics. He put on his glasses with the clip-ons, Thoughts stung his mind, feeling like wasp stings. *That prize is worth nothing to me. I worked nonstop for a decade on that problem with light. They'll use it as a weapon. No one loves me because I won it.*

He noticed that he was muttering out loud, "Stop it." His thoughts continued; *People envy my Nobel Prize. Say I'm the great scientist. Bull. Will anyone remember me in a thousand years? I can't even remember who won the 1918 prize in Literature. Whoever did is dead, decayed, gone.*

Quite suddenly, Rokko noticed the experimental notes he had been writing up. *I'm a respected scientist. I'm proud of it. This is important work,* he thought. Suddenly, he realized he was playing a role completely opposite to the one he'd been playing a few seconds before. *I've got to take these glasses off.*

Rokko was dizzy. He swayed and, after about forty seconds, fell to the floor. On the ground he cried out, "What the hell have I made?" He closed his eyes, and the unbearable oppression stopped, but now a new thought came, less overwhelming but even more depressing, *What am I doing with my life and why? What should I be doing?*

His wife of twenty-five years, Nina, heard Rokko's call from her upstairs office. She rushed down, took his left hand in hers and asked, "What's wrong, dear?" Rokko briefly thought of having her try on the glasses. *I love her. Why torture her?* he thought. He grabbed his right calf and said, "All of a sudden, I got a tremendous pain. Please get me some ice."

Rokko opened his eyes and watched as his wife jogged towards the kitchen. *She doesn't really believe me, thinks I'm hiding something,* he thought. *I wonder if she still loves me.* The panic attack started again. *I don't want to know. I'm afraid to know. I'm a coward.* He slipped the clip-ons off his glasses and carefully put them in their crushproof case and hid them under his desk. He struggled up to the chair in front of his desk, pulled himself up. His wife returned, with a bag of ice, looking concerned. She was surprised when Rokko first held the ice to his forehead and then to his calf. Rokko saw the questioning look and said, "A pain in the calf is also pain in the brain."

"Yes, dear. Maybe you've been working too hard lately."

"You're right. Let's go to Saint George Bistro tonight."

"With pleasure. I'll make a reservation. Are you OK?"

"I'm fine," said Rokko. Nina left. Rokko sat at his desk, holding the ice first to his leg and alternating it to his forehead. It was very refreshing.

At the restaurant, Nina asked him why he'd been so tense lately.

"Overwork. I promise to relax." He ordered a bottle of Sancerre.

"A bit extravagant tonight."

"Anything for you."

"Then tell me why you called out, 'What the hell have I made?'"

"You must have misheard me," said Rokko. "I said, 'What the hell have I done,' thinking about the pain in my calf."

Rokko could see a look of doubt cross Nina's face. "If you say so," she said. Rokko changed the topic, something he was very good at.

The next morning, he was in his office at the college, and he thought about the glasses he'd just made. *I must be the first person to experience this in two millennia.* He wanted to test the mirror. He got it out and looked at himself for ten seconds and then closed his eyes. His experience was the same, but it wasn't quite as much of a shock this time.

Rokko came up with a plan. He'd ask Audrey if she'd try the glasses. Next, he'd approach one of the philosophy professors in his college and, finally, a religious person; he was thinking of someone who believed in the examination of conscience. He realized he had mixed motives for doing these experiments. Yes, he was a scientist, but he was mostly doing this for his own glory. *I should tell them what they're getting into but that might ruin the experiment. I don't want to hurt them, but I've got to know the truth.*

Rokko hadn't spoken to Audrey in over six months. The exhibition had been successful, and she'd written a book on the expedition. When they met in the faculty lounge, he asked if she'd done any more research on the mirror. Her head shook, almost as if she was surprised that he'd asked. "No. I've never had the time." He explained that he had fabricated both a mirror and glasses just like the mirror they'd put away and asked if she'd be willing to try them.

"I don't think so."

"But you'd learn something about ancient Greece and how they might have used the mirror."

She shouted, "I said, I don't think so." She paused and looked around. One of their colleagues was looking at them. "Sorry, just blurted that out."

Rokko changed the subject, and they chatted for a few more minutes. After Audrey and the colleague left, Rokko looked at himself in the mirror. He saw himself playing a part, pretending to be Audrey's friend, when he just wanted to find out how she'd react. He quickly closed his eyes and put the mirror away.

Rokko thought of the definition of a philosopher in ancient Greek; one who loves the truth. That didn't describe most of philosophy professors at the college. They were too concerned about their reputation for brilliance.

Rokko began to think of individual professors. There was Midi Henderson, the Marxist philosopher who wrote praising the dictatorship of the proletariat. Rokko didn't like Midi or her ideas. They would mean everyone on earth would become the slave of a dozen or fewer individuals who thought they knew everything.

Rokko was pretty sure Midi wouldn't want to see that she was playing a role. He'd have to fool her into putting on the glasses. That would be fun, but the next time Rokko looked in the mirror, he'd see himself playing a role of complete surprise when Midi inevitably got angry. Rokko would suffer if he persisted with this plan.

Rokko thought of the professor he nicknamed Harmless Horace. At thirty-five, Horace Jute was the youngest, tenured full professor on campus. He was very popular with the students. He had recently written a bestselling book, *Bliss Exterminates the Illusion of Pain*. For the first time, Rokko noticed his true feelings about Horace. He had the fierce desire to hit Horace with a stick until he agreed that in this world pain was real and had a purpose. Yes, Horace was the ideal philosopher to try the glasses on. He called Horace, who agreed to meet him in Rokko's office the next day.

Horace came in wearing sandals, a T-shirt, and blue jeans. He hadn't shaved in a few days and the stubble was rather becoming. They chatted for a few minutes. Rokko showed Horace a photo of the inscription and asked if he read ancient Greek. He didn't. Rokko described what they'd found and asked if he'd take part in an experiment. Horace agreed to allow Rokko to do a video recording. Rokko set up a digital camera and started to record.

"Tell me about your philosophy of life and living." Horace gave a two-minute speech about bliss obliterating this illusion of a world. Rokko could feel his own hands begin to involuntarily make fists. Horace continued to talk about happiness, honesty, honoring others, kindness, and how the differences between people were trivial. Rokko thought, *I'm so glad it's him and not me who has to look in that damned mirror.*

Horace stopped talking. Rokko handed him the mirror. Rokko saw Horace's hand began to tremble as he held it. Rokko tried to hide his inner smile. *Am I becoming pure evil?* he wondered.

Horace gazed into the mirror. He began to weep and dropped it to the ground. He sat there, breathing deeply. His right-hand tore through his hair.

"What did you see?" asked Rokko.

"It's very personal."

"We're friends," said Rokko, who felt pain at telling this lie. "I've looked at it myself, so I'll understand."

Horace insisted that the camera be turned off. "You won't tell anyone will you?"

"Of course not," said Rokko, with a pang in his heart. He knew he wanted to publicize this.

"I tell people to delight in this safe, embracing world. I don't believe that. I'm obsessed with my career, in making people love me. There are so many people I hate." Horace shook his head and put his left palm on top of his right hand, which was on top of his head.

Horace got up and started to leave. He turned around and said, "You promised not to tell anyone. You must destroy the record of this experiment."

"Maybe we could do this again sometime?"

Horace didn't answer and left.

Rokko deleted the computer file, knowing he could restore it later, if he dared. He was pretty sure he wouldn't dare.

Rokko was in despair. *These glasses aren't helping anyone. Even I don't want to put them on.* He began to think of his younger brother, Xavier, whom he hadn't seen in several years. Xavier was a Brother in the Order of The Hermits of St. John. The order resided in a rural area, which was a two-hour drive from where Rokko lived.

Xavier had joined the order when he was nineteen. Their parents were opposed because Xavier was a brilliant student, well-liked by everyone in his classes.

"You won't learn anything real there," Rokko had said to Xavier, over twenty-five years ago, before he joined the order. "You'll be following an illusion. Why bury yourself?"

"If a man will begin with certainties, he shall end in doubts, but if he will be content to begin with doubts, he shall end in certainties."

"Quoting Francis Bacon. It's absurd and pathetic." Rokko saw he'd hurt Xavier's feelings, but he didn't care. Twenty-five years later, Rokko still thought that Xavier was wasting his life and talents.

The hermits grew flowers that they used to make perfume, which they sold, along with collecting donations, to support the order. Rokko drove to the hermitage. He saw Xavier pruning rose bushes. He was wearing a black habit, rosary beads swept down to his waist, which had a simple black cord around it. He wore inexpensive shoes. When he walked, Rokko noticed that there was a hole in the sole of Xavier's left shoe.

Rokko stood in front of Xavier. He always did this, expecting or perhaps only wishing that Xavier would greet him by name, or at least make a gesture of recognition. That never happened. The order had strict rules that a hermit could only speak if spoken to first. Rokko wondered, for the hundredth time, why couldn't he accept that simple fact? He then had a disturbing thought that maybe he did accept it, and he was just playing a role that he couldn't step out of.

"Brother Xavier," Rokko said. "I'd like to talk to you."

"Yes, my friend, how can I help you?"

"Don't you recognize your own brother?"

"All humans are my brother or sister."

"Cut the crap Xavier." Rokko felt uneasy. *I say that every time. I've never noticed.* "Can we go someplace to talk in private?"

"Not quite private, but there are rooms where hardly anyone ever comes." Xavier walked into a stone building and down a short corridor. There was a door on the right. Xavier opened the door. There were three chairs on each of the walls and a small stained-glass window high up on the back wall.

"All these chairs," said Rokko. "I thought you never spoke to each other."

Xavier didn't answer.

Rokko explained why he was there. He wanted to see if Xavier would either put the glasses on or look at himself in the mirror.

"What's their purpose?" asked Xavier.

"The mirror allows one to see oneself clearly, if one has the courage to do so. The glasses allow us to see oneself and other's thoughts. Well not exactly thoughts, maybe roles ... It's really hard to explain. Try it, I think you have the courage."

Xavier took the mirror in his hand and looked at it. Rokko remembered that both Audrey and Horace's hands trembled when they held it. Xavier's hand was calm. Xavier looked directly into the mirror and didn't say anything. Rokko noticed he was smiling.

"What are you seeing?" Rokko asked.

"What I always see when I examine my conscience. It took me over a decade to be able to do so and not tremble."

"You mean you've seen this before?"

"Not so directly or so continuously," said Xavier. "It's wonderful."

"Would you have any use for such a mirror?"

"It would be an invaluable gift. We could have novices look into the mirror and see if they are suitable." Xavier fell silent and then continued, "But that might not work."

"Why not?"

"One needs to be prepared, persistent, and willing," said Xavier. "Willing to see what one doesn't want to see, or it would be a plague, a torment." He paused and then continued, "A great deal of training would be needed to make it useful. But for the serious, you have made a wonderful tool. Let me try the glasses."

Xavier put them on and looked directly at Rokko. "You're thinking that just maybe I've learned something. You're even a bit proud of me?"

Rokko reluctantly said, "Yes."

Xavier took the glasses off. "Have you been using them?"

"Yes. When I can. It's much harder than I thought. Would you like me to make you a mirror?"

"Yes, but our order is dying out," said Xavier. "We haven't had a novice in four years. I'm afraid you'll have to learn how to use this difficult gift by yourself unless you want to come here to live for a while."

"You know I can't do that. I'll see what I can learn on my own. Are you going to recognize and greet me next time I come?"

"You know the answer to that."

"Yes, I do." There was a long pause. "And quite right too."

Rokko left, not knowing how or if he would use the glasses or the mirror he'd made. Perhaps it was best to just pack them up like the first expedition had done. On the drive home he began thinking. *No. I've got to go on. Before, I didn't see all the roles I'm playing and how I couldn't step out of them. That ignorance seemed like bliss.*

When he got home, he made coffee for himself and Nina. Rokko was pretty sure Nina wouldn't enjoy looking in the mirror, but she'd asked, multiple times, what he'd been working on so hard. As they dunked their biscotti, Rokko started to talk. "Some people say or feel that ignorance is bliss." Rokko could see Nina squinting her eyes. Rokko continued, "I've decided that ignorance is just ignorance."

"I have no idea what the heck you're talking about."

Rokko smiled. "I'm not sure I do either but let me try to explain."

"I'll listen with the greatest pleasure."

He explained as best he could and gave her the mirror. "Best to wait until you're alone to take a look. I'll be in my office in case you want to talk." He walked to his home office down the hall. He sat down. He felt afraid. A minute went by. He heard nothing.

Two more minutes. Nothing. Rokko was relieved.

The sounds of "Rokko, what the hell have you made?" blasted down the hall. *Well, this is going to be interesting*, was Rokko's first thought. His second was, *I should have packed them up and put them in storage.*

He got up and raced to the kitchen. Nina was on the floor, holding her calf. "All of a sudden, I got a tremendous pain," she said. "Please get me some ice."

Rokko got her a bag of ice, which she put first to her head and then to her calf. "A pain in the calf is also a pain in the head," she said.

Rokko didn't know if he should, laugh, cry, talk or remain silent. Neither did Nina. Neither said anything. They looked at each other for a long time.

Rokko waited; worried and curious.

"Ignorance is just ignorance," said Nina. "Let's leave it for now."

"I didn't mean to hurt you."

"I'm tougher than you think," said Nina. There was a pause, she shook her head and added, "Maybe."

Rokko went back to his office. He felt himself trembling. He hadn't realized how precious his marriage was to him or how fragile it might be. "Ignorance is just ignorance," he remembered Nina saying. Then he thought of what he'd said to Xavier, "Try it, I think you have the courage." He should apply that saying to himself, but Rokko realized that he wasn't like his brother. He wasn't exactly a coward, but he didn't want to go on with the experiment.

On the other hand, he'd already let at least four people know about or use the glasses. He couldn't back out now. *I'll have to pretend to be brave, h*e thought. *That's not very positive*, he heard himself thinking. *This is from a man who won a Nobel Prize?* He heard himself cry out, "I am brave."

He was startled to look up and saw Nina, who was standing in the doorway looking at him. She still had the ice bag to her forehead. "Yes, you are, dear. I wanted to remind you of the three projects I promised to finish this year. I'll leave this one to you." Nina walked away.

Rokko felt relieved. *One fear gone,* he thought. *Thousands more to go.* He searched for the mirror and looked in. Twenty seconds later, he closed his eyes and put the mirror away. *I am brave. I am brave. Well, at least a little.*

MR. OMNISCIENT

I hate Mr. Omniscient.

It's 8:30 a.m. and Mr. Omniscient (his name is really Jason) begins yet another absurd story. "I worked in Germany for two years. The food there has no preservatives so you can eat and drink as much as you want and never gain weight or get drunk. Every morning, we'd each bring in a six pack of beer and down one every hour. At lunch we'd each drink a liter of wine. No preservatives, so we never gained an ounce or got drunk."

I've seen fat Germans (no offense intended), so this has to be BS, but I've learned not to argue with Mr. O. Not much anyway. Disagree on the minor points. Not that Jason ever changes his mind or admits he doesn't know something, no matter how obscure the topic. But – and this is a big but – he_is tall, extremely thin and although we often each drink a quart, or more, of beer at lunch, he never shows the slightest sign of inebriation or of gaining weight.

There are eleven computer programmers in our obscure section of the brokerage firm. Our boss, Tim Neary, goes to lunch at ten and comes back around four smelling like a sour IPA. When you ask him a question in the morning, he replies, "Ask me after lunch." When you ask him when he comes back, he answers, "Ask me in the morning." Mr. Omniscient often says, "I love Tim Neary, as long as he's not near me." This always gets a laugh from the programmers, even from me.

The big boss is named Henry. Henry has four teams, like ours, working for him. We release new computer code to production every second Friday. Henry sets our goals based on the theory that no problems will come up. They always do and we're often late. On the Wednesday before release, Henry gathers us together and asks each person individually if they'll complete their goal on time. If a person says they aren't sure, he says that the new features have already been announced to the users. Every program needs to be completed on time. "Failure to complete means termination."

On Release Fridays, Henry sits at his desk and plays with his little plastic four-inch axe that he's named Ethelbert the Executioner. He waves it in the air and says "I hope I don't have to use Ethelbert today. Ethelbert is ever ready." Henry always axes an individual at five o'clock. He wants to get a full day's work out of his victim before he fires them.

It is Release Friday and my project to build an index isn't finished. I look over and see Ethelbert in Henry's hand and Henry's eyes on me.

At 5 p.m., my boss and Henry come over to stand at my desk. Jason and the rest of the programmers stand and look on. My boss says to me, "You failed."

"I ran into problems," I say.

"Doesn't matter," says Henry. "You broke your personal promise to me. Besides Ethelbert is hungry."

Mr. Omniscient interrupts. "I don't know, Henry."

"What don't you know?"

"I don't know if that's fair."

"I'm always fair," bellows Henry as he raises Ethelbert the Executioner over my head.

"Let me show you something," says Jason. "To create the index, you must use the instruction 'BUILD-IDX'. It doesn't work."

Henry, my boss, the other programmers and I watch as Jason types in the command "BUILD-IDX" and points it to my dataset. He hits enter and a message, "Failure 157484" comes up.

"It happens every time," says Mr. Omniscient.

Henry looks over at my boss.

"Why didn't you tell me about this problem?" My boss asks me.

I lie. "I did. On Monday and Tuesday."

"I don't remember that." My boss replies.

"It was at 1 p.m. when you returned from lunch," said Jason.

My boss turns red and says, "Yes, now I remember."

My boss, Henry, and Ethelbert the Executioner don't notice all our successfully hidden snickers.

Ethelbert is put away. "Fine," says Henry. "Have it ready for the next release." He and my boss leave.

"Jason," I say. "You know that instruction works."

"Yes, but if you have a plus sign in the data, it fails. I merely put a plus sign in your data. Those idiots will never know. I think Ethelbert the Executioner is the smartest of the three."

"Thank you, Mr. Omniscient." I blush and correct myself, "I mean thank you, Jason."

"How could I let the one person who argues with me get fired?" he asks with a smile.

I love Mr. Omniscient. I mean Jason.

Once You've Crossed, You Can't Come Back

"Governor," said his aide. "It's a bridge too far." The two were sitting in the governor's office.

"What the hell are you talking about?" asked the governor. "Don't do it. You'll regret it."

"Why shouldn't I sign the death certificate and get the execution over with?" the governor asked with a scowl on his face.

"You've been out of the state running for President. I don't think you really understand. Right after doing the murder, he pointed the gun at his head and shot himself. They found him dying. They operated on his brain. He's not the same person. He's now completely childlike."

"He killed in cold blood," said the Governor. "Don't you remember."

"Yes. It was brutal. You asked me to interview him. The person who sits on death row is not that killer. That person is gone."

"The jury voted for death."

"You legally must review all death penalty cases," said the aide. "The legal and ethical requirements for clemency are there. You can commute to life in prison."

"So now he's sorry about what he did? Is that it? It's not good enough."

"The man you sent me to see – well, he's not really a man anymore. He's not even a boy. He doesn't know his own name."

"That's ridiculous. He fooled you."

"There's no cunning in him. I've interviewed all the jailors. They agree to a person. He's thought of as an obedient child with a mental age of about four. He tries to help everyone."

"I'm running for president against a man who is known to be tough on crime. I'll lose votes if I commute. I'll probably lose the election."

"Your opponent doesn't have to live with executing a young, helpless child," said the aide. "You do."

"You haven't convinced me."

"What does it gain a man to have the whole world and lose his soul?"

"Don't quote that to me," said the governor, with passion. "I have so much to offer this country. I'll make a much better president. I don't want to hear another word about it."

"Did you hear what I said? I said he doesn't know his own name. I called him Mike the first time, and he responded and didn't correct me. Next time I called him Tim and he just smiled and told me what a wonderful breakfast he'd just had and asked if I'd play cards with him. He wondered why he's kept away from the others. He doesn't even know he's in jail."

"I didn't fly here to grant clemency. I'm going to sign the death certificate and leave."

"Don't cross that bridge," said the aide. "Once you've crossed, you can't come back."

"Shut up. I've made up my mind."

"You'll be forcing people, who know they'll be killing a little child, to do something evil. Do you know what that will do to them?" The aide was thinking but did not say, *and do to me*? He continued, "Don't do it. For their sake even if not for your own."

The governor turned his head to look at a photo on the wall. He said nothing.

"Go interview him yourself," said the aide. "You'll see what I'm saying is true."

"That's enough. My decision is made."

"I got permission to be there during the execution. I'll write you to tell you about it."

"Don't bother," said the governor. "I'll be busy campaigning." The aide left the governor's office.

A few weeks later, the aide wrote to the Governor.

Dear Governor,

I want you to know what the person you called a brutal murderer did on his last day of life. They asked what he wanted for his last meal. He asked for hot dogs with sauerkraut and chocolate cake. I asked the warden if I could bring it to him. He said yes.

A minister and the prison warden were there with him. As they left, they told me that they'd told him he'd be executed at sunset but that he didn't seem to understand.

I brought the tray in. He smiled. He offered me one of the hot dogs saying he liked to share and besides you shouldn't eat too much before an operation. "They're going to cure my forgetfulness," he said.

He saved the cake saying he'd eat it when he got back. "Always good to have a treat after you see the doctor."

We each ate a hot dog. I could barely look at him. I smiled and tried to hold back tears.

I asked if he was afraid?

He said, "Afraid? Why? They're always good to him here."

We then played "Go Fish". He wasn't any good at it. He asked me if I had any fours, three times in a row. He was never upset when I didn't have any. When he was down to his last card, I asked if he had any sixes. He smiled and said, "Great you picked the right number." He was happy that I won! He asked me why I was weeping when I just won the game?

After half an hour, they brought in the gurney, and he sat on it. He helped the doctor find the best vein for what he called the medicine. He asked me if I'd come back to eat the cake and play cards with him when the operation was over. He said he'd play better then. They strapped him down.

Before they put in the poison, they asked him if he had any last words.

"Last words?" he asked. "No, I'll have something better to say tomorrow."

I am very sorry that he's gone.

When the governor was handed the envelope, he put it in his jacket pocket without looking at it. Later, in his hotel room, he opened it, read the first paragraph. He shook his head saying, out loud, "What's done is done." He threw the letter in the wastepaper basket.

At The Wedding or Haikus and Our-kus

When Peter got to Miryam's Orthodox Jewish wedding, he saw his co-worker, Yana, who was Miryam's younger cousin. He called out but she kept walking away from him. Peter was guided into a roomful of men. Two men were loudly speaking to each other in Hebrew. Peter didn't speak Hebrew, so he didn't understand what was being said. Abe, his co-worker, who was also Miryam's older cousin, whispered in his ear that the two people talking were Miryam and the bride's fathers. They were negotiating the terms of the wedding contract. He wondered why Miryam wasn't involved with the discussion.

Peter knew he should have studied Orthodox Jewish wedding customs, but he'd been completely preoccupied with his private life. He wondered if he should be here. Maybe he should just leave. He had never met Miryam's fiancé, and he didn't want to do so now. He felt like screaming but didn't dare. He hated scenes. His mind drifted and he began to think of how he'd met Miryam and gotten invited to her wedding in the first place.

Peter was a twenty-five-year-old Catholic, Italian American. He had worked as a computer programmer with Miryam and her cousins, Yana and Abe for the past eight months at the computer center of a large savings bank. There were eleven programmers who all worked together in one large white room with bright florescent lighting.

Peter's first job had been programming teller machines in different cities across the country for a large computer manufacturer. He'd recently gotten a new job, at a New York City bank, because they were installing these new teller machines, and they needed an expert to help them. He was extremely happy to be back working in the city permanently.

Peter considered himself to be very talented programmer until he started working for Abe. He quickly realized that Abe was a far more talented programmer than he was. Was it because Abe had been doing it for twenty years? Peter had originally thought so, but that illusion didn't last more than a week. The speed at which Abe picked up the new software was astounding.

Miryam, who was a year older than Peter, was assigned to help Peter test his programs since she knew the bank's systems well. He soon realized that she too was a faster learner than himself. It was rather humiliating. He'd been used to being at or near the top of any enterprise he'd worked on.

One day, Abe said to Peter, "I already told you how to do that."

Peter had wanted to say, "No you didn't," but held back. When the conversations ended, Miryam who had been listening, said to Peter, "I bet he didn't tell you."

"How do you know?"

"He does it all the time," said Miryam. "Either tells you way too much or forgets entirely. I tell him when he's wrong. You should too. Don't worry. Abe's said some good things about you."

"That's surprising."

"He's really not that bad. Talk back to him." She paused and added, "Respectfully."

"Got it." Peter realized that he was attracted to her, not that he was going to do anything about it. They lived in entirely different worlds. But the eyes and mind are connected to the heart and his heart gave a little flutter.

The company had a cafeteria. Free food for lunch and coffee breaks were included for all employees. There was a choice of a few main courses, salads, desserts, and beverages. Miryam, Abe, and Yana brought lunch from home because they ate a stricter brand of Kosher than the cafeteria offered.

Every day at lunch, Abe would play and quickly beat another programmer at chess. Peter ate with a few other programmers. Yana and Miryam would usually sit together in a corner.

They also had two coffee breaks per day: one in the morning and one in the afternoon. These could be taken whenever the employee wanted to do so. Miryam and Yana usually went together, both drinking their coffee black.

One day, when Peter entered. Yana and Miryam were sitting at a table near the back. As Peter was getting his coffee, he heard Yana say to Miryam, "A dead ringer."

Peter asked if he could join them. Miryam smiled and said, "We've been waiting for you."

"I heard you say, a dead ringer. Who's a dead ringer?" asked Peter.

"It's the punch line of a joke," said Yana.

"I don't get it," said Peter.

There was a pause and then Miryam said, "What's a doorbell that doesn't work?"

Peter shook his head back and forth.

"No need to laugh," said Miryam.

"Guess what?" asked Yana.

"What?" asked Peter.

Yana, chuckled and said, "Miryam's getting married."

"Congratulations," Peter said.

"Thank you," said Miryam.

"When's it to be?" Peter asked.

Miryam looked into Peter's eyes and said, "Five months."

There was a silence and then Yana said, "Miryam has only one invitation left, and she wants to invite you."

"Are you sure, you want to use your last invitation on me?"

"I'm sure," said Miryam.

Peter said yes. He asked if he'd know the groom. Miryam said that his name was Isaac Levita, from Baltimore. Peter didn't recognize the name. As Yana and Miryam walked back to their combined office, Peter heard Yana repeat, "A dead ringer."

From that day on, Miryam and Peter drank coffee together during their morning and afternoon breaks. Occasionally Yana joined them but mostly they sat alone. At lunchtime, if Peter was too busy to go to the cafeteria, Miryam would always notice and bring him some food.

One morning, Miryam mentioned that she wished she could write poetry. Peter said that in high school they'd been given an assignment to write haiku, a seventeen-syllable poetic form.

"I wasn't able to think of anything," Peter said, "until our teacher read us *A Poppy Blooms*, by Katsushika Hokusai. "I write, erase, rewrite / Erase again, and then / A poppy blooms."

"That's great," said Miryam. She counted on her fingers and said, "but it's not seventeen syllables, it's sixteen."

"Maybe in Japanese it's seventeen," said Peter. "They're supposed to be lines of five syllables, then seven, then five but my teacher wasn't that strict."

"Tell me your first one."

"Are you sure you want to hear it?" asked Peter.

"Of course."

"Six eagles took flight / five white heads flew to the west / one flew east, alone."

Miryam counted the syllables on her fingers and said, "You followed the rules. Were you the one flying alone?"

"Sometimes."

"I fly alone too sometimes."

"It's not very profound." Peter said.

"It was your first one," said Miryam. "I think we should both give it a try."

"Why not? Peter asked. "Let's try tonight and then we'll share tomorrow."

That night, Peter wrote and erased and wrote again to no avail.

The next day, at coffee, Peter asked Miryam to read her haiku.

"I'm a little embarrassed," she said.

"Why?" Peter asked. "Is it terrible?"

"It's not that. I don't expect much from a first try."

"Just say it then," said Peter.

Miryam read, "Come see my treasures / My captivating eyes glow / Never fading hence."

Peter immediately wondered if Miryam had written this for him or for her future husband. He wished it were for him.

"Let's hear yours," Miryam said.

"I got nothing."

She looked closely at Peter. "What's that paper in your pocket?"

"I wrote something but it's awful."

"Just read it."

Peter read, "It is a haiku I say / that tells me nothing /about your sweet self."

Miryam counted on her fingers and then said, "That's sixteen syllables. Change the word 'sweet' to 'loveable.' That makes seventeen and it will be a proper haiku."

"It's not in the five, seven, five format," said Peter.

"It's seven, five, seven. Not orthodox but why does that matter?" asked Miryam.

"So now we're going to allow five, seven, five and also seven, five, seven?

"Seven, five, seven will be our own literary form," said Miryam. "We'll call it an our-ku."

"Our-ku? What the heck is that?"

"Our own brand of haiku," said Miryam. "We're in charge of our own world. We can write either haikus and our-kus."

"People will laugh at us."

"Doesn't matter if we like them," Miryam said and smiled looking into Peter's eyes. "Listen to how it now sounds, 'It is an our-ku I say / that tells me nothing / about your loveable self.'"

Peter laughed. "Sounds great. I agree. We can write haikus and our-kus."

"If I wasn't so sure you'd never do anything wrong," said Miryam, "I'd think you were flirting with me. Was that poem for me?"

Peter blushed. "Of course I wrote it for you." He stopped and then continued, "That's what we agreed on, isn't it."

"Yes," agreed Miryam. "Poetry's a bit flirty. Let's do it again."

The next workday was Monday. Peter had spent almost the entire weekend thinking of a haiku. He thought he'd come up with a good one. Was it too suggestive, he wondered?

People usually had coffee around 10 a.m. Peter and Miryam went at 9:30 a.m.

"Where are you going so early," asked Yana.

"We finished what we were doing, we thought we'd go now," said Miryam.

They went to the cafeteria, got coffee and sat in the back, far from the windows and lunch counter.

"What did you come up with?" asked Miryam.

"You first," said Peter.

"I went first, last time. Your turn."

"Ladies first," insisted Peter.

"That would be cheating. You're not a cheater, are you?"

"Of course not." He blushed. His mind was already half a cheater. He couldn't vouch at all for his body.

"Go for it," said Miryam. Peter sipped his coffee.

"I'm waiting," said Miryam.

"Forever starts never / beauty is as beauty does / dazzling eternity," said Peter.

"That's beautiful," said Miryam, "but it's a bit cliché. What do you think of mine?" She took a slip of paper from her handbag and read, 'This coffee is hot / I sip it so cautiously / Not like love inflamed.'"

"My coffee's a bit hot too," agreed Peter. "That was a haiku. I've thought of a new one. Here goes. 'Smile then look away / Pretend you don't care at all / No one else will know.'"

Miryam was smiling. "That one's hot too," she said. "We probably shouldn't do this every day. We'll never get any work done."

They agreed to share them once a week. The next time Peter was set to start. Before he did Miryam said, "Read it with passion. That's what real poets do. And you want to be a real poet; don't you?"

"Sure," said Peter. He smiled and read in his most seductive voice. "You ask me what I'm typing / Fingers flying fast / A love letter. What else?"

"Wow. Maybe I can top that. 'I pat my empty pillow / Waiting for your cheek / Please come, lay yours next to mine.'"

Peter looked around. "I'm glad no one heard that." Miryam pointed with her eyes. Peter turned his head to see Abe standing less than ten feet away.

"He's my cousin," said Miryam. "He won't say anything."

"But he'll think …"

"Yes. He'll think we're poets," said Miryam. "Isn't that what we are?"

For the first time in Peter's life, he began to think seriously of marrying. He'd met many women he liked or lusted after, but Miryam was the first he thought would make a good wife, someone who interested him intellectually, whom he felt comfortable with, and one he'd like to be around in difficult as well as happy times.

But Miryam was an Orthodox Jew and Peter was a believing Catholic. If they were to marry, there seemed to be only two choices: either Peter or Miryam would need to convert. Peter doubted that Miryam wanted to convert, and he was pretty sure that if she did, her family would shun her. That's what Yana said happened to her cousin. They'd sat Shiva, the ceremony for the dead, when she'd left the faith. That's a very high price to pay for conversion, even if one wanted to do so, and Peter didn't believe that Miryam would want to do so.

Peter wondered if he could convert. Of course, he could but could he do it good conscious? To turn his back on Jesus, whom he loved? Perhaps to be able to think of Jesus as a good person but no more? Could he do that? He didn't think so.

If he'd been born into a different family, he'd have different beliefs. He'd been to Venice where his maternal grandparents were from. They had lived on a narrow street where the apartments almost met. There had been two ornate churches nearby and five blocks away there was the ancient Sinagoga Levantina. If things were a little different, his great-grandmother might have attended that synagogue and he'd be Jewish.

Peter began to fantasize that perhaps they could marry secretly and pretend they both were still single, but it wouldn't work. He wanted children and he knew Miryam did too. Besides, Miryam certainly wasn't in love with him, or was she? He often saw her looking at him while he worked with what seemed to be love or maybe it was lust.

One day, he was shocked when he heard one of the other programmers ask Yana if he and Miryam were having an affair. He was thankful that Yana said, "No", with great conviction.

Finally, it was the week of the wedding. Both Yana and Abe asked Miryam why she continued to work right up to the wedding. "You should take a few days off before hand," said Abe. Miryam told him that she and Peter intended to complete their project before she left for her honeymoon.

At 5 p.m. on the last day, as she left the office, Yana told Miryam that she should leave too. Miryam ignored her.

At 6 p.m., Abe left, urging Miryam to also leave, to make sure she got some rest for the wedding tomorrow. Miryam replied, "Peter and I still have some work to do."

Around 7 p.m., Miryam went to the employee refrigerator and got out a sandwich for each of them. They ate. "I bet there are haikus you were afraid to read to me," Miryam said.

"Maybe one."

"Let's hear it."

"It's not appropriate," said Peter.

"A bride can demand a gift. Let me hear."

"It's an our-ku."

"Out with it," said Miryam.

"You asked for it. Here goes. 'Red flatters you, as does blue / Green and orange too / But you'd look best in nothing.'"

"Hot. I've got one too. Ready?" asked Miryam.

"As ready as I'll ever be."

"I know you love me / Let's share one kiss now / While we still have time."

"I can't," said Peter. "It's not right."

"I kiss my grandmother," said Miryam. "Sharing one little kiss can't be all that wrong."

"One little kiss?"

"One little kiss," said Miryam. "I'm not married yet. Just one tiny, little, nothing kiss."

"OK. One tiny kiss."

"I don't want anyone to see," said Miryam. She took Peter by the hand, and he gladly followed her to the cleaning closet.

Once inside, Peter kissed her, somewhat chastely on the lips. She put her tongue in his mouth. Miryam broke the kiss and said, "Your kiss inflames me / Hurry. Put it in me now / Over and over."

"Five, seven, five," Peter said, trying to change the direction of events, "It's a proper haiku."

Miryam repeated the haiku with a slight difference, "Your kiss inflames me / Idiot. Put it in me. / Over and over."

Not surprisingly, nature took her course. When they were satiated, Miryam said, "Thank you Peter. I'll never forget this gift."

"It was your gift to me too," said Peter. They got presentable and left.

With the end of re-imagining that scene, Peter's revelry ended. He was back at Miryam's wedding ceremony, where the wedding documents were being prepared, before the wedding ceremony. Abe asked as he was shaking his shoulder. "Did you fall asleep?"

"Just daydreaming," said Peter. "What happened?"

"It's all settled."

"What were they arguing about?"

"What happens if there's a divorce?"

"Do you expect a divorce?" asked Peter.

"You'd know that better than anyone. They were arguing what happens if there are no children."

"Why?" asked Peter.

"Isaac's an only child. So is his father."

"What are you saying?"

"Think about it," said Abe.

"Where do they come from?"

"The family lived near the Sinagoga Levantina in Venice until around 1900.

"That's near the Campo San Leonardo."

"I've never been to Venice," said Abe.

"My great-grandparents lived not a three-minute walk from there."

Later, at the wedding ceremony, the couple was under a canopy with Isaac in the center. Miryam, veiled, circled him seven times as prayers were said. Peter couldn't keep his eyes off Isaac. The question, "Who is a dead ringer?" repeated over and over in his mind. *Not a dead ringer*, he thought *but not too far off either*. At the end of the prayers, Isaac crushed a glass with his foot, and the crowd cried out "Mazal Tov."

Abe whispered to Peter that the crushed glass symbolized the destruction of the Second Temple in Jerusalem.

"I think I'll go now," said Peter. "I'm not feeling well." He wasn't lying.

Peter awaited Miryam's return from her honeymoon. He wanted to talk. He was shocked when a week later Abe told him that the Isaac and Miryam had decided to move to Baltimore.

"His family runs an extremely successful business there," said Abe.

Miryam didn't call or write. Peter thought of going to Baltimore to see her, but he didn't think it was a good idea. If she wanted to see him, he was sure she would make the first move.

A month went by. Peter was moping. He wrote a few haikus and our-kus but didn't enjoy them. He overheard Abe talking to Yana, "I didn't think he could do it."

"What are you two talking about?" Peter asked.

"Great news," said Yana. "Miryam's pregnant already. She cracked a joke, "Some people get busy quick."

Peter got up and walked quickly to the bathroom to stop himself from crying.

"What's got into him?" Yana asked.

"Can't you put two and two together?" Abe asked.

"What?"

"I'd bet ten to one …" Before Abe could finish Yana whispered, "Shut up Abe. Don't say that. Ever."

"You're right," said Abe. "Sometimes I talk too much."

Miryam had a baby girl. Peter figured out that the baby was born thirty-five weeks after the wedding. "They did get busy," he tried to tell himself.

Peter continued to accumulate haikus and our-kus. A year later he decided to send them to a literary journal, *Haiku Today*. In its latest issue, there was a haiku written by a Miryam Levita.

"Our baby smiles / And each time I think of you / Far away not here."

Peter went to his notebook and read one of the first our-ku's he'd written for Miryam but had never read to her. "You glance in my direction / I hope you do see / My thrill of recognition."

He sat and wrote another one. "I turn the doorknob and push / To see what's inside / Surprise. There's life of both sides."

He sent both to *Haiku Today,* but they were not accepted for publication.

Rock Breaks Scissors

I've been waiting for my friend Ernest for fifteen minutes. He texted that his bus arrived on time. I texted back, "See u soon." My text was delivered. It's late September with bright sunshine and a slight breeze.

I watch a man on Madison Avenue walking towards the Morgan Library & Museum. *I hope it's him.* There aren't many people walking around at 10:05 a.m. on a Sunday morning, so it probably is. The walker is about the right height, weight and age but he turns left. It can't be him.

Ernest and I talked twice last night to make sure of our arrangements to meet at The Morgan on 38th Street and Madison Avenue at 10:05 a.m. The bus was to arrive at the Port Authority Bus Terminal at 41st Street and Eighth Avenue at 9:50 a.m. Google maps said it should take twenty minutes to walk over. I've walked it in ten.

Ernest walks a bit slower than me so I told him he could do it easily in fifteen minutes. He should be here shortly.

Twenty minutes. The Morgan is a wonder, built by the richest man of his time. He collected everything from five-thousand-year-old Fertile Crescent ceramic seals, which astound me with their beauty and modernity every time I see them, to the most modern paintings. Ernest had never been to The Morgan, and I looked forward to showing it to him.

I'm not sure what the special exhibits are today, so I stroll to the huge exhibition posters. One exhibit is rare manuscripts of flora from the fourteenth century and the other is paintings and drawings from nineteenth century France.

Maybe, I should have met Ernest at the Port Authority, but I have a slow healing sprained ankle and I'll be walking around all day. It's much safer to only walk the few blocks from Grand Central station and meet him at The Morgan.

Twenty-five minutes. Why was he so late? Maybe he picked up coffee? I text again. The text isn't delivered. Why?

I think about our friendship and rivalry of almost forty-five years. I remember that silly game we always played to settle our disputes. We both shoved out our right hand at the same time, signaling either paper, rock or scissors.

It's easy to tell the winner. Paper covers rock. Scissors cuts paper. Rock breaks scissors. What was hard was deciding which symbol to choose. Only God could win every time. I envied that ability.

Ernest had three brothers and three sisters, and both his parents were teachers. I had a brother and sister, and my dad was a janitor; my mom was a homemaker. I was a bit jealous about that, but he had a pet turtle. I had a pet dog. A dog beats a turtle any day. Paper covers rock.

By our junior year, we were neck and neck with Lorraine in the race to become the valedictorian. He was tops in English. I was far behind. I was tops in mathematics. Ernest was quite a way behind. Lorraine was second in these and tops in several others. She was a universe ahead of us in one category. She was beautiful and the most popular girl in school. I'd tease Ernest saying I'd beat him for valedictorian, but I would never tease Lorraine. I had a year's long crush on this girl who, except for politeness, barely acknowledged I existed.

I got a job in my senior year, working thirty hours a week, besides doing my schoolwork. Neither Lorraine nor Ernest had a job, and they forged ahead. Lorraine won. She went off, on a scholarship to Princeton. I dropped out of college at the end of my first year. Ernest got his Ph.D. He never brought up that I didn't even have a bachelor's degree, but I felt the implied status gap. I'd gotten a job by going to a trade school to learn computer programming.

Fifteen years later I went back at night school and got my BA. There was no equality there. He was a full professor. His rock broke my scissors.

Twenty-nine minutes. He's got to be nearby. I think of walking up 38th Street towards the bus terminal to meet him. But if I did, and he was walking on 39th Street, I'd never find him. One of us had to stay in one place. Besides, my ankle hurts, and I still had all day to be on my feet. I call him. It immediately goes to voicemail. I leave a message to call me.

Thirty-one minutes. I text again. The text isn't delivered. Could he be lost? No. He's visited New York City lots of times. I'd sent him exact directions. Walk from 41st Street down to 38th. If you're going the wrong way, you'll hit 42nd Street you'd turn around. At 38th Street, take a left turn and continue straight. The museum takes up the whole block so you can't miss it when you get to Madison Avenue. I'd sent him the names of the avenues he would pass through and told him that if he hit Ninth Avenue he was going in the wrong direction, so just turn around. They're the simplest directions in the world. Maybe he'd gone off in the wrong direction twice, which would help explain why he was so late.

Thirty-four minutes. A group of students asks if I'd move so they can take a group photo in front of the library sign. I move and see someone coming towards the corner. It can't be Ernest. He's much too tall.

I think of a previous get together from about five years ago. I'd gotten married many years before, but Ernest never did. We were having a late lunch at a small café near the Whitney Museum. The place had almost cleared out. Our waitress, Joann, was a cheerful woman, a few years younger than we were.

Ernest complained to me, "I can't believe I can't get a date with someone who has at least a BA. I'm a full professor at a distinguished university. Why can't I find an educated woman to go out with me?"

"There must be lots of women you can date," I said.

"I live in Podunk Pennsylvania. Sure, there are cashiers and cleaning ladies, but what would we talk about?"

"Everyone has interests. Just because you don't think they do doesn't make it so."

"Do you have any idea how much effort it takes to get a Doctorate?" he asked.

"Do you have any idea how much effort it takes to mop floors?"

"Good one…" He laughed and was silent and then went off to the men's room.

He'd be spending a few days in Manhattan. I wondered if I could get him a date or at least cheer him up. Joann came by. I told her that my friend was having a hard time and wondered if she'd flirt with him a bit. She said she was married and was not that kind of a girl.

I apologized hoping I hadn't insulted her and then said she'd be doing kindness by getting Ernest talking and laughing. She smiled but said nothing.

Ernest came back. He was wearing a shirt with his university name across it. Joann came over and started talking to him saying that her sister had gone there. Ernest smiled and asked where she'd go to college. I headed off to the men's room. When I came back, they were still chatting.

Ernest hadn't even asked her to have a cup of coffee with him. No wonder he never got a date. He asked me if I'd asked the waitress to chat with him. "Of course not," I lied. I'm not sure he believed me. Happily, he was more cheerful for the rest of the day. Since that time, he's never mentioned going on any dates.

Thirty-eight minutes. Maybe he called me, and my phone is having a problem. It has three bars, so it's not likely. Perhaps, by mistake, Ernest had called me at my house. If he had, my wife would have called me to let me know. Maybe she had called, and my phone wasn't working. I think about calling my wife to ask her advice about what to do but I don't want her to worry. It hasn't been that long yet. Maybe he had to go to the bathroom and stopped at a restaurant. There are rest rooms in the Port

Authority and here at The Morgan. It's only a short walk. He should be able to wait that long. You never know though.

Forty-one minutes. I walk into the museum, in case, miraculously, I'd missed Ernest. Of course, he's not there. I think of stopping a cab and driving around looking for him. What if I'm not here and he shows up. It would be complete confusion.

I think of high school. In our junior year, we'd been on the volleyball team. In our first game, our team was down eleven to two when the coach called a time out and told us we were the better team and should win easily. I didn't believe him. The other team served the ball at Ernest. He jumped higher than I'd ever seen him and slammed the ball back over the net. It hit the ground with a loud thwap. Scissors definitely cut paper on that one. We went on to score the next seven points in a row and won the match. Our team won every game that year. It was my only championship. I still remember that sweetness almost like s'mores covered with honey.

Forty-five minutes. I take out my phone to dial 911 and then stop. Is someone really missing if they're a half hour late? They'd probably laugh at me. I text again. It doesn't go through. I dial the "9" and stop. I'll give Ernest more time.

I see a man walking down Madison Avenue, a block away. The man was in an army uniform so it can't be him. The man reminds me of our long-standing rivalry in Risk, that board game to conquer the world. We'd play it with another of our friends. What is there about pretending to conquer the world that brings out a bitter rivalry between people? Or was the intense feeling of rivalry only in me? I felt the rivalry. I'm not sure either of them did.

In the game Risk, the players take turns picking countries. We divided up the countries we considered to be traditional enemies. It was always Yakutsk versus Irkutsk, or Egypt against the Middle East. We'd put enough armies in each so that these traditional contests would drag on and on.

I enticed my rivals to fight each other, while I concentrated on sealing off some area of the globe to get extra armies on each turn. In this game, my paper continually covered rock as I won twenty-seven games in a row. I was surprised my two friends never caught on, nor did they ever seem to get angry at losing. I would have banged my head against the wall if I'd lost two games in a row.

Fifty minutes. I go into The Morgan and get our tickets. It only takes three minutes. I go back outside but there is no one walking within a block of the museum.

Fifty-four minutes, I call 911 and hang up when a woman answers. What if she asks for a picture of Ernest? I look on my phone. Nope. I'd unloaded my photos last month. Should I ask my wife to send me one? I still don't want to worry her. How could it hurt to wait another few minutes?

Fifty-nine minutes. I call Ernest again. Voicemail. Where could he be? If he hadn't texted me, almost an hour ago, I'd assume his bus never arrived. I'm cold. I stand just inside the outer heavy door of the museum, breath slowly and look out. I can't stay inside. I'm too nervous. I have to go out and look for Ernest again.

I remember that fifteen years ago, Ernest got hit by a car while crossing the street. Perhaps he's been hit by a car today. Maybe he's in a hospital.

I think of our senior year. Neither of us had found anyone to go to the prom with. Finally, only a week before, I asked a girl I'd met the previous summer. Ernest didn't find a date. I thought, paper covers rock.

A few weeks later, Ernest and I went to see Miss Universe at a local mall. We were second in line to say hello. She was beyond attractive. She thanked us for coming to see her. We were no one and she was the Universe. What humility and grace. I don't how to express it. We both won that day.

Sixty-five minutes. Still no Ernest. I again think of our rivalry. I was practicing to become a baseball pitcher. In the summer of our junior year, we were playing baseball at a local park. He was a left-handed batter. I so wanted to strike him out. It would have been rock breaks scissors. My fourth pitch was down and in. His blast went over my head, over the fence. There was a forest beyond the fence. We searched but never found the ball. Maybe it's in orbit. I've seen stranger things happen. His rock broke my scissors that day.

Sixty-eight minutes. I break my daydream and walk to the corner to look up 38th Street. There is a doddering man, with washed out, messy hair, about half a block up. He is about the right height, but it couldn't be Ernest. He's walking far too slowly. I walk across the street. My breath, which I must have been holding involuntarily, gusts out. It's him.

I get closer. Ernest doesn't notice me. Probably I look older too. My ankle is sore but I'm walking three times faster than he is. We're a few feet apart. He still doesn't notice me. "Ernest," I call out. "I'm so glad to see you." Ernest, who is looking down at the sidewalk, looks up but there's no immediate recognition.

"It's me," I call out again. Ernest shakes his head, as if to vanquish a daydream.

"Wonderful to see you," I say.

I reach my hand out. Ernest shakes it and says, "Hello." His legs are bowed out a bit. His hair is spiked out, not due to design.

I blurt out, "I'm so relieved. I thought you'd have been here way sooner."

"This is the best I can do these days."

I ask why he didn't answer his phone. He says it never rang. I call him again and his phone doesn't ring. I have him call me and my phone doesn't ring either. A few seconds later, someone calls my cell phone and it rings. It's so odd but somehow, today, such odd occurrences are almost expected.

We walk to The Morgan. I wonder if he knows how slow he's been. Will I slow down like that in the next year? Is this the last time we'll see each other. I have lots of mental questions but no answers. I want to ask Ernest how he got so decrepit in the last year? I don't ask. He mentions that his younger brother died last month. "So sad to hear." I remember that his brother had prostate cancer.

We go inside and see the illuminated manuscripts of herbal plants. Ernest had studied illuminated manuscripts and was extremely impressed. "Do you have any idea how exceptionally well made these are?" he asks.

We talk about his work, his health, his thoughts, his siblings. He tells me his youngest sister is having troubles with her boss and his oldest sister is having trouble with her marriage. I ask a lot of questions.

We go into the West Room. The tapestries, the paintings, and the collection of the first printed bibles fascinate him. I point out a Hans Memling painting, but he just walks by it unnoticing. Why am I judging him for that? You can't notice everything at The Morgan. There are hundreds of items in each room.

At lunch we talk about his teaching assignment.

"Tell me?" I ask. "How are your classes going?

"I'm having trouble with my chairperson," He answers. "She keeps telling me I should retire."

I wonder if this worry is why he was walking so slow earlier. "Do you want to retire?" I ask.

"Of course not. I love teaching."

"So did you tell her that?"

"Yes, but then she suggested I go into semi-retirement, give up half my classes."

"What do you think of that?"

"They'd only pay me a quarter of my salary. I don't want to do that."

"Can they force you out?" I ask.

"They can make it damn uncomfortable. I'm overworked. No one should have 123 students."

"Why so many? Is she setting you up to fail?"

"The chair screwed up the schedule. I'm only teaching intro courses. There are forty in an intro compared to ten or twenty for other courses."

"Think it's intentional?" I ask.

"Could be. She started hinting about retirement a whole year ago, but I should have checked the schedule myself before it was finalized but I didn't."

"So it's your fault too?" I asked.

"Partially."

"Why is having intro students so hard?"

"I give three quizzes each semester each with three essay questions. Do you have any idea how much time it takes to give good feedback on all of them? It's awful."

"You could give a multiple-choice test."

"In college?" He shouts. He stops and continues in a more normal voice, "That's high school stuff. You might as well not be in college if you're going to get multiple choice tests."

"I had some college classes with multiple choice questions," I say. "To do well you really have to study."

"I will not compromise."

"You're not going to let her push you out, are you?"

"Not if I can help it."

"Never give in," I say. "Don't let paper cover rock." He smiles, remembering our game.

We go to the French painting exhibit and continue talking. During the whole time we've been there, he never asks me a single thing about my life. Nothing about my wife, children, work or health. I'm not surprised or upset.

His bus is at 6:20 p.m. I ask him if he wants to take a cab, but he wants to walk. I offer to walk with him even though my ankle aches. He says he'll walk on his own. At 4:45 p.m., he starts to walk towards the Port Authority. Strange to say, he no longer looks old to me. What seems entirely so different and unusual in the morning quickly becomes the new base standard and looks completely normal by three. I walk to Grand Central and take the train home.

That night, I text asking if he got home safely. He texts back, the next morning saying how much he loved the library and how glad he was that I had introduced him to it.

I wonder if we'll see each other next year. I realize that in the ultimate Rock, Paper Scissors game, only God, or, if you aren't a believer, only life itself, has that ultimate choice in that matter.

I think about Ernest. Why do I think of our relationship as a rivalry? I want to be more supportive. Still, if it was possible to go back in time, I'd go back to that baseball game and try like hell to strike him out. If I did, I'd think rock breaks scissors and gloat silently. I'd be lying if I said anything else.

"I SHOULD REPORT YOU
BUT OFFICIALLY I NEVER
SAW ANYTHING"

Said Sarafina Rodriguez to Pete Hermitage as they watched the Director of Human Resources making her way towards them. Sarafina and Peter were both managers in the Sales division.

Peter remembered yesterday's manager's discussion, led by this HR director, concerning improper conduct between an employee and a manager. "We have a zero-tolerance policy. No abuse of power by management, in any form, will be tolerated. All incidents must be reported. If you see any incident, however small, report it. Failure to do so will result in termination."

Peter put his hand up to ask a question about reporting.

Another person was first. "What about a spontaneous display of affection initiated by the employee?"

"That's just another way of saying an abuse of power," said the HR director.

If I ask another question, I'll be getting between a momma bear and her cubs, Peter thought. *It will never happen to me.* He lowered his hand.

The next day, at the start of the holiday party, Peter said to Sarafina, "This DJ's great."

"Sure is," replied Sarafina. Peter could see that she was softly swaying her hips to the music. The two had worked together for seven years and each year they'd danced together at the party.

"Want to dance?" Peter asked.

"Nope. You'll notice that José isn't dancing." José was their Vice President of Sales.

"He's always the first one out. Maybe he isn't feeling well."

"Or maybe he wants to continue to feel well," said Sarafina.

At that moment, Veda, who worked for Peter, came up. "How about asking me to dance?" Veda looked expectantly into Peter's eyes. Peter noticed Sarafina's eyes giving him a warning not to accept.

"Maybe later," Peter heard himself say. Veda grabbed his hand and pulled him onto the dance floor. Most people were dancing either by themselves or in groups. Veda held Peter's hand as they danced. Suddenly, Veda pulled Peter to herself and planted a long, lingering, liquid kiss on his lips. Perspiration cascaded down Peter's back. She smelled enticing like jasmine, honey, and alcohol. Her lips were soft. Peter thought he felt a touch of tongue. He knew he should pull away strongly and immediately, for all to see, but that would be extremely rude. He didn't want to embarrass Veda in front her friends. He was enjoying the kiss. When it ended, Peter noticed many people watching them and smiling. A few even clapped their approval.

When the song ended, Peter said, "Thanks for the dance," and walked over to Sarafina.

"No one's kissed me like that in years," Peter said. "Theoretically, I should report her, but I don't think she should be disciplined for that."

"You're right," said Sarafina. "You'll be. They'll say you have the power and enticed her to dance with you."

"Power? Me? I couldn't even ask the HR director a question and you're a witness, Veda asked me." They saw the HR director walk towards them.

"Looked like a spontaneous display of affection to me," said Sarafina. "I should report you but officially I never saw anything."

As the HR director got closer, Peter noticed fire in her eyes and two hands raised, fingers extended, like bear claws. She stood next to them. Almost a minute passed in silence, punctuated with searing looks from the director. Finally, she broke the silence. "Ms. Rodriguez, I just gave you the opportunity to report Peter to me. Both of you should report to my office tomorrow by nine." She left them.

GRYTHOMORESOME

James, forty-one, a one hundred seventy-five-pound nurse with thick black hair, was sitting in the group meditation hall at the Full Awareness Meditation Center, which was situated in a rural area on a fifty-acre property, that included a large forest with walking trails. This was the first day of James' first meditation retreat. The retreat would last for ten days. He had been so nervous lately. A friend had guaranteed him how overwhelmingly peaceful a silent retreat would be. He decided to give it a try.

It was almost the end of the last sitting meditation of the day. James lost track of the meditation and began to daydream. Six months ago, he had been in his basement carpentry workshop with his nephew, Phillip, twenty-six, a short, broad faced man. The two men were making bird houses to place on the trees around James' and his neighbor's yards. James picked up his portable, re-chargeable nail gun he'd bought a few days before. It fit so easily in his hand. He'd asked Phillip, "Have you ever used a nail gun?"

"Nope," replied Phillip. "Never liked carpentry much."

"That's because hardly anyone can nail straight. It's simple using a nail gun. You might start liking making things. Let me show you."

James had already cut the pieces of wood to the correct sizes. The birdhouse would be about a foot long and about ten inches square around. He'd clamped one of the boards in his vise, held the other in place and nailed the side, effortlessly shooting in four thin nails. "See how easy that was. You try."

James clamped another board down and handed the nail gun and another side to Phillip, who picked up the nail gun, looking at it admiringly. They re-clamped the boards so that they could nail another side. James held it to the board and pressed the trigger. The nail went in clean and perfectly straight. He shot in three more nails. "It's so easy," said Philip, with a broad smile.

Then Philip said, "You know, I've been thinking. You haven't invited me down for ages. Why today?"

James' daydream then turned to what his five-year-old daughter Kylse had said to him, ten days before that. They'd been playing tag in the yard and James had said, "I have a secret, I've never told anyone. When I was your age, I had a Martian friend, who seemed so real. He came from a long line of warriors. The gravity on Mars is much less than on Earth so his body was almost seven feet tall and very narrow. He had a high piercing voice. He never cut his stringy hair, and it hung, in a rather tasseled state down his back. He always carried a long iron spear in his right hand. His name was Grythomoresome, and he bragged that his name was much more interesting than mine."

"He's right," said Kylse. "Yours is boring. His is great. What did you do together?"

"He tried to train me as a warrior. It was hard. I mostly failed. He also appeared when I was in trouble or doubt like the time when my friend kept beating me at Scrabble."

"'Your friend is cheating,'" Grythomoresome said.

"'Can't be. He's completely honest,'" I said.

"'How do you know?'" he asked. That was one of his favorite questions.

"I said, 'I've known him for years.'"

"'Known him for years? So what?'" Grythomoresome laughed. Strange to say, his laugh was low in his throat and deep, quite unlike his speaking voice. He said, 'Pretend not to look but watch when he picks up new letters.'"

"What happened?" asked Kylse.

"My friend looked at the bottom of a letter and put it back and took another one. I was going to call my friend a cheat, but Grythomoresome warned me it might not be a good idea."

"Why not?"

"On Mars, it is a grave insult to accuse someone of cheating. They may challenge you to a duel. 'Much better to prevent crime, if one can,' he said, 'Then no one gets hurt. Watch him as he takes the letters and make sure he notices you watching. He'll get the message without having to accuse him. Always think carefully before you act. Dishonesty is rare on Mars but is so common here on earth.'"

"How wonderful to have someone who can tell you if someone is lying," said Kylse.

"It wasn't wonderful when he'd ask me if I was fibbing especially when I fibbed to myself. He always seemed to know."

"I don't need imaginary friends. I've got plenty of real ones."

Abruptly, James' daydream snapped. The lights of the large meditation room had been turned down and the hundred meditators had begun to chant the Buddhist precepts in Pali. He read the translation as the first precept was chanted. "I promise not to destroy the life of any creature be they large or small."

He felt something crawling on the back of his left hand. *I can feel that bastard walking through my hair, looking for the perfect place to plunge its beak in. I hate mosquitos. Why do they always bite me and no one else?* There'd been a severe outbreak of West Nile Virus in the area and seven had died.

James raised his right hand to crush the mosquito. Time seemed to slow down. *This mosquito might infect me or someone else. Maybe it's better to kill it.*

James lowered his right hand. *I just promised not to destroy life. I won't strike the damned pest.* Instead, he shook the mosquito off. James hoped he'd done the right thing.

The last official activity of the day was the walking meditation. Each person walked back and forth across the room trying to fully experience each footstep. James went to his favorite walking room, which was below ground, with one tiny window almost at the ceiling. There was a granite Buddha statue on an altar at one end. The window was so high up and the wall lights were so low that the room was almost dark. You had to wait for your eyes to adjust before you started walking. Perhaps this was why it was so rarely used and why James liked it. He was alone. He started to slowly walk back and forth. He could feel each time his foot touched the ground. He walked back and forth three times, before the images of the ending of his meetings with Kylse dominated his consciousness.

"I've got a secret too," Kylse said to James. "Phillip taught me a tickling game, but he told me never to tell anyone about. I don't know why. You know I like to tickle people."

"Yes, and you're ticklish too," said James.

"Phillip said there were some places that were really nice to tickle, and he had me tickle him there and then he tickled me in the same place."

"Did it tickle?"

"No but it felt good. I didn't know there was something so large in his area. I don't have anything like that there."

"How often have you played this tickling game?"

"Must be at least three times."

"I don't remember inviting him."

"He works half a day on Wednesdays. He comes over before you get home."

The images were so real that James stumbled and fell to the floor. He crawled to the side of the room. He was breathing hard. What was he supposed to do when his daughter told him this? He hadn't known. If he went to the police, she'd be questioned and then have to testify and that would be horrific. James was a nurse. Maybe he should steal some poison and kill Phillip? That should be easy enough. No, killing is immoral. He thought about what Grythomoresome had said about stopping crime before it happens. He'd stop Phillip. There had to be a way.

James' mind returned to the rest of the birdhouse-building scene.

Phillip held the nail gun up and said, "This nail gun is wonderful. I love it."

"I thought you would," said James. "I paid cash at Home Depot. Cash is completely anonymous. The clerk said everyone's buying one. It's portable, you can use it anywhere."

"I can see why it would be popular."

"And think how useful it is." James paused, looked directly into Phillip's eyes. "Supposing someone was molesting your daughter. She'd already been hurt. You wouldn't want her to have to go to court. Instead, it would be the easiest thing in the world to meet that person outside, in some lonely place, and put the nail gun to their head and pull the trigger. Nail guns aren't registered."

Phillip cowered but tried to stand tall. "Yes, I suppose that would be a solution to a problem like that …."

"But if the offender stopped and I mean not just hurting one person but entirely stopped, well it wouldn't be necessary. Would it?"

"I agree entirely."

"Don't ever come to my house again when I'm not here."

This scene kept running through James' mind. He tried to stop it by thinking of something pleasant. Each time, his thoughts went back to Kylse and Phillip. At home, James could turn on the TV, read a book, shot some hoops, talk to his wife, have a beer or two but here there were no distractions. No talking, reading, writing, drinking, hanging out. Even looking directly at others was discouraged. It was just James and his escalating, explosive thoughts. As soon as he succeeded in stopping one horrible image, three new ones sprang up in its place.

James fell to the ground and then looked around. There was no one else in the basement walking meditation room. He knew it was forbidden but he called out, "If I told Grythomoresome about my friend's guarantee that I'll have a peaceful ten days, he'd have asked me 'How do you know that's true?'" There was no answer, but James felt slightly better.

It was time to sleep. He went to his room and lay down. *They'll ring the gong at 5 a.m. to start another day.* He didn't fall asleep for what seemed like hours.

Gong, Gong. The bell ringer pounded the large bronze bell at the end of his corridor. Four minutes later, as he felt the hot water of the shower fall on his head. James mumbled, "I swear, I'm going to get my thoughts under control today."

The first sitting meditation was easier than the day before. The work period came after breakfast. James was assigned to wash the dining room floor, which took two people to complete. They could only complete the task by working as quickly as they could. It was a relief. James only thought of Kylse and Phillip a few times.

Within two minutes of beginning the seated meditation, intense images of Phillip crowded James' brain. James was mentally no longer in the meditation room; he was reliving the past.

In the second week of November, James had come home and found Kylse muttering to herself. When he asked what was wrong, she said that Phillip had come over. She'd told Phillip that he wasn't supposed to come over when James wasn't there, but he said you'd changed your mind, and he could come over We argued. He didn't leave until I kicked him hard in the leg.

James was in a fury, but he tried hard not to show his anger either to his wife or Kylse. *It's not so bad. I can deal with this. I'm going to scare him at his house.*

James began to consider how he could meet Phillip without anyone noticing. He was a member of a gym that was about a mile from Phillip's house. There were cameras when you came in and out, but he knew of a side exit without a camera. The door locked behind you if you left that way. He could leave, put something in the door to prevent it from closing, see Phillip and then come back. It's dark by 5:15 p.m. when Phillip gets home. He lives by himself, on a deserted lane. James could park a block from the gym, leaving the nail gun in the car. James imagined himself holding the gun up as Phillip arrived. That would scare him. Maybe he'd pull the trigger to shoot a nail in the air. Maybe not. Yes, he'd scare Phillip. Phillip was a monster. There was no telling how many others he'd been abusing. A criminal doesn't stop with one crime.

On the way home that day, James drove to Phillip's place and found a little place nearby to park the car where it couldn't be seen. There was only one streetlight two hundred yards from Phillip's house, so it would be dark. If he timed it right, the whole operation shouldn't take more than twenty minutes. James believed it was damned good plan. *He'll be scared and never do it again.*

The next day not only did James make sure the camera saw him as he entered the gym, but he also said hello to the woman at the front desk. At 4:45 p.m., he slipped out the side door, making sure he propped it open, so he could get back. He got to his car in two minutes. By 5 p.m., he was crouching behind a low hedge besides Phillip's door. It was dusk but he could still see in the twilight. A few minutes later, he heard a car parking. It must be Phillip. James held the nail gun in his right hand.

Suddenly, James heard a pounding on the ground right next to him. *What the hell is that* he wondered. He looked to his right and he saw the legs of Grythomoresome. "Warriors don't hide and spring on their victims unaware," said Grythomoresome. "They show themselves."

"Shut up," James said out loud. He heard Phillip say, "What the heck."

James stood up. He had his arm outstretched with the nail gun pointing at Phillip, who was standing a few feet away. He saw James, turned and ran to his car as fast as he could. James watched as Philip sped down the road.

Twenty-five seconds later, James heard a crash and saw flames in the distance.

James walked to his hidden car and started the engine. He drove in the direction opposite to the flames, back towards the gym by an alternative route; He thought he'd gotten clean away.

Grythomoresome was sitting next to him. "A warrior doesn't run," he said.

"I'm no warrior," said James.

"You're being a coward." James turned around and drove back towards the fire. He stopped a few hundred feet from the light pole where Phillip's car was burning. James could see a burnt body sitting in the driver's seat. He called 911. A patrol car came quickly, followed by an ambulance and a fire truck. The flames were almost out when the fire truck arrived. Perhaps Phillip had been almost out of gas.

The police questioned James, who said he was driving to lend his nephew some tools when he saw flames. He explained that James' house was about a quarter mile down the road.

"He was coming home from work?" asked the police person.

"Yes. He gets out around now," said James.

"So, why would his car be going in this direction?"

"I don't know," was all James would say.

When James got back into his cars, he heard Grythomoresome say, "Looks to me like you're glad he's dead."

"What?" James asked out loud. He became aware he was actually sitting in the meditation room. He remembered the meditation directions, "Follow the anchor of your breath and then you can expand the consciousness outward." He tried but was soon back into the chaos of his emotions. The thoughts "I'm a killer. Yes, I'm a killer. No, it was a tragic accident," just wouldn't go away.

On the second day, James and eight other people meet with one of the retreat leaders. On day five, James would meet individually with the eighty-five-year-old revered master meditation teacher.

The meditation leader, who was about James' age, asked if anyone was having any serious difficulties. James said he had a hard time keeping in the present. The leader talked about her first three-month retreat where she'd been tortured by the thought that she had no money. She said that, by the end of the retreat, this thought had decreased.

James almost shouted, "It took three months for that trivial thought like that to fade? Shit. I helped kill someone. I'll be dead before that thought fades away." Instead, he said nothing.

The next days were an endless struggle. James imagined he was a rat running on an electrified spindle, going round and round, getting nowhere, being shocked with every step. Twice, he thought he heard Grythomoresome, standing next to him, pounding the butt of his iron spear into the floor. He was very happy that Grythomoresome hadn't shown up. That would make this nightmare retreat even worse.

Finally, James had his interview with the eighty-five-year-old master meditation teacher.

"How are you today?" the master teacher asked with a very deep voice, much more forceful than James expected. He spoke slowly, with great precision.

"I have a very active mind," said James.

The master teacher laughed. "You are blessed to notice that. Most people have no idea."

"But my thoughts and my actions are…" James stopped talking.

After waiting a long time, the teacher continued, "Recognize what you're experiencing. Accept it. Investigate it. Practice non-identification. Your thoughts are not you. You understand that don't you?"

James felt like yelling, "What the hell is non-identification. I've killed someone. What do you know about murder?" Instead, he was silent.

The master teacher waited. James said nothing. One tear slowly dripped from his left eye.

Finally, the teacher said, "I'm an old man, who will soon be gone. I promise I will never repeat what you tell me. There is nothing I haven't heard. What is your pain?"

Suddenly, James noticed that Grythomoresome was standing to the side of the teacher, looking directly into his eyes.

"Tell me," said James. "We chant a precept not to kill even the tiniest of living beings. If a mosquito lands on my leg and I believe it has West Nile, do I shoo it off, so it bites someone else, or do I kill it?"

"I've urged them to mend all the screens in the meditation room."

"Wonderful evasion," laughed Grythomoresome. James ignored him.

"What happens if I do something bad, like kill the mosquito?" asked James.

"We reap the rewards and punishments of our actions. I do not believe that you are this disturbed because you killed one mosquito."

"I can deal with killing a mosquito," said James. "What if we killed or wanted to kill a human being? Doing it possibly to save the innocence of a child?" James told him the whole story.

"That is serious," said the master teacher. "If I give an answer, meant only for you, will you keep silent, never to repeat what I say while I'm alive?"

"I promise," said James.

"When I was in training, we had a meditation master who molested young students. He was so greatly admired that not only was he never accused, but also no one would ever have believed it was true. I knew better. Every spring, we had an initiation on a high mountain retreat. Three new monks were up on the mountain. The Master and I were traveling together to meet them. As we walked, I told the Master I knew what he was going to do. He never even pretended otherwise. He said he would be imparting his spiritual power to them."

Grythomoresome said, "Ask him the name of this master." James again ignored him.

The teacher continued, "There is an abrupt rock face right before the initiation place. It started to snow hard.

He said we should go back to the shelter a half mile below. I said I was very sure footed. I went ahead, got past the spur and reached to pull him up. I grabbed his wrist, started to pull him and then opened my hand. He fell to his death. No one ever suspected me. Did he deserve to die for molesting young monks? I don't know. What about me? I will get my reward or punishment. I am indifferent to it. I can sit, meditate and let it be."

"It's easy to claim to be indifferent," said Grythomoresome. "If the story is true and he's indifferent, why keep it secret?"

James again ignored Grythomoresome and asked, "How could you have done that? You're revered as a saint."

"There are no saints, only people who strive to improve," said the master teacher. "No, it is we killers, who know what we are capable of, who can make the most progress. We have no illusions. We know we have much to do, much to change, much to let go of. Do you think you can go now, sit and seriously try to meditate and just ignore the past?"

James heard the pounding of an iron metal spear. Grythomoresome asked, "Can anyone ignore the past?" and then spat on the ground.

"I don't think I can do that," said James. "It would not be good to just forget."

"For most people, that advice is enough. But not for you… Or for me."

"You still obsess about that moment and feel the pain?" asked James.

"Often and always at retreats."

"What do you do?"

"I declare a truce for the whole retreat. During the truce I give myself permission to meditate. I promise to let those thoughts come back later."

"I'll try it. I'll declare a truce for this meditation retreat."

"Go with my blessing."

After the interview, James sat in the meditation room and, for almost five minutes, he was able to follow his breath and keep in the present. After ten minutes, James was again swimming in his thoughts. James heard the beating of an iron spear against the floor. He looked up and saw Grythomoresome who asked him, "Do you believe he murdered that man?" He laughed his deep laugh and continued. "I can't imagine him stealing even a single grape."

James said out loud, "I'm sure you're wrong. Every word he said rang true."

From the next cushion there came a sharp whisper, "We're not allowed to talk. You're disturbing me. Please be quiet."

James stopped talking. Grythomoresome whispered, but his high piercing voice seared into James' mind, "He said call a truce for the entire retreat. If you could do that, you wouldn't need a retreat."

James said out loud, "What do you suggest?"

"That you shut up" came from the woman sitting behind him.

Grythomoresome continued to laugh. "When I tried to train you, did we do it twelve hours a day?"

"No."

"You would have died. They have you meditate twelve hours a day here. You can't do that."

"What do you suggest?"

"That teacher's advice wasn't terrible," said Grythomoresome. "Declare a truce for half an hour and meditate, then come play with me in the woods." He left.

James declared a truce and was able to concentrate for fifteen minutes before he began to remember Phillip's burning corpse. He sat for another five minutes and then ran off to the woods, saying, "I'll declare another truce when I get back." Grythomoresome was waiting for him.

TOUCHDOWN

Joe, wearing a torn football jersey, shorts, and a baseball cap that covers his greying hair, looks at the wooden bookcase that is against the wall of the small living room of his apartment, where he lives alone. It must be moved before the wall can be painted. Everything else is ready: the unopened paint can, the paint pan, and roller, as is the plastic that he plans to stretch to make sure the paint doesn't get onto the floor.

Moving the bookcase is the hard part. The bookcase is five feet tall and four feet wide. He removes mostly paperbacks and a cookbook on diabetic cooking, a recent gift from his neighbor Terry. He hobbles to put them in boxes in the middle of the room, walks back and continues the operation. It takes more time than he thought it would. His right leg aches. "Damn. I'll sit after I've moved it." He wonders when he began to talk to himself, something he'd always thought of as a sure sign of madness.

Finally finished, he starts to slide the bookcase first on the right side and then the left leaning against the wall to brace himself from falling. The bookcase moves a few inches each time. Hopefully the floor won't get scratched. On the fourth move he grabs onto the top almost falling over. Feeling slightly dizzy, he shouts out, "I will not stop."

He finishes moving the bookcase and puts the plastic down. He goes to the kitchen where there's a warm pot of coffee. He drinks a cup and smokes.

He goes back to the living room. There is a short stool near the paint pan, because he isn't sure that he can kneel to pour the paint and then get up. He pours, gets up slowly and begins to roller paint onto the wall. It's slow work and he almost trips a few times. He finishes and takes another break.

Joe is drinking coffee when the doorbell rings. He opens the door and Terry is there. Twenty years ago, they played high school football together. Terry played right tackle, and Joe was the star running back. "Come in," says Joe. They go to the kitchen, sit down. Joe pours Terry a cup of coffee. They chat for a few minutes.

"Didn't think you still had your jersey," Terry says.

"Still fits," says Joe.

"Mine doesn't," says Terry. "Let's move the bookcase."

"Already started painting," says Joe.

"I said I'd come over and help."

"Decided to do it on my own."

"What?" asks Terry. "You could injure yourself."

"I'm fine."

"They just cut your lower leg off. It's the first time you're walking on that fake leg. You've got to be cautious."

"I am cautious," says Joe.

"You're crazy."

"Come look."

They walk to the living room and Terry sees that Joe had completed the wall. "I'll help you clean up," says Terry.

"You mean you'll watch me clean up," says Joe.

Joe pours the remaining paint back into the can, closes it and hobbles back to the sink to rinse the roller and pan out. He finishes, sits down and then removes his artificial lower leg which ends below the knee in a flat area covered with a skin graft. Some blood is oozing out of the base.

"Not bad," Joe says. Terry looks and then quickly turns away.

"What did you expect?" asks Joe. "There's bound to be some problems."

"You should have let me help."

"I told you I'm going to do everything I did in the past," said Joe. "I won't change just because they cut my lower leg off."

There's a long pause. Joe takes care of the bleeding and puts the prosthesis back on.

Joe smiles at Terry. "You can look now. Tell me how I did?"

Terry slowly shakes his head back and forth and then jumps up. He raises his hands straight up over his head and shouts out, "Touchdown."

Joe smiles and says softly, "I thought you'd approve."

A Tiny Pebble

There was a message on my voicemail again this morning for the ninth day in a row. "What's wrong? You don't call me anymore. Pick up. I know you're there. It's Lorraine. Call me back."

I didn't return her call. I don't have any idea what to tell her. I could tell her the truth, but I'm embarrassed to do so. We've been best friends for five years. We talked about everything. Why can't I tell her? Why can't I mention what happened to Mandy? Her fate haunts my imagination.

Maybe something's the matter with me? I want to tell her what I'm feeling but I simply can't. Not this time. Last time we talked, I said a bit but nothing really personal. From a rational point of view, I can't even explain it to myself.

Let me write it out. Then maybe I'll understand. My name is Maria. I'm twenty-nine, married, with one child, Carol, a thriving eight-year-old who talks about becoming a famous pianist. My husband George is the superintendent of our apartment building. It's an old building with fifty apartments and lots of cranky tenants. I work in an insurance agency in Manhattan in the East 50s.

Five years ago, I went into the Spirit Bookstore, which is on the same block as my agency. It's a small bookstore that sells new age books. I walked by for years and had absolutely no interest in going in. The week before, my mom had been diagnosed with breast cancer. Her mom (my grandmother) died of cancer, and I was worried. (Knock wood. She's in remission.) I tried to convince myself that all would be well, but it's so hard to have faith when you really need it. It's much easier to believe when everything is going well.

The idea of knowing the future suddenly appealed to me. Some people say the tarot can give you a hint.

The bookstore was down a few steps and the cashier was sitting behind the counter. I looked around and there was no one else in the store. There was jasmine incense burning and the lighting was subdued. I'm sure they thought it made a more spiritual atmosphere, but I felt slightly ill at ease. I saw bookcase after bookcase with topics like Buddhism, Tarot, Divination, Health, Proper Eating.

The shelves with tarot books were so densely packed that I wondered if only magic prevented them from collapsing. I noticed what appeared to be a simple book, with a title something like *Tarot in Two Shakes of a Stick*. What a pretentious but immensely humorous title. I reached for it.

"Sorry," I said, as the back of my hand hit another hand. A thought flashed through my brain that I should move to another section. I was afraid the person might wonder what I was looking for. Who wants to admit to a stranger that you want to know the future?

Before I could move, I heard, "Sorry. It's my fault. What book were you trying to get?"

I looked up and saw a woman, who seemed about fifteen years older than me. She had very short black hair, a rather boyish face and a friendly smile. She was dressed in blue jeans and a blue work shirt, and she wore sandals. I told her which book I was reaching for.

"What a fantastic coincidence. We must have a lot in common that we'd try to grab the same book at the same time."

I laughed an embarrassed laugh. She suggested we get a cup of coffee.

I looked at my watch. "I'm supposed to get back to work now."

"We'll make it quick. I like making new friends. My name is Lorraine."

"But I'll be late."

"Don't be embarrassed. A little break before you go back will do you good."

"How do you know I'm embarrassed?"

"You're breathing through your mouth. If you felt at ease, you'd be breathing normally."

The comment made me laugh so we went to Starbucks, and to my astonishment, there was no line. I was beginning to believe in signs and that seemed like a good omen. It turned out that Lorraine and I did not live very far apart from each other, near Prospect Park in Brooklyn. She said, "I love biking down the big hill to see how fast I can go."

"I like that hill too but I'm always afraid to go too fast in case I fall off."

"You probably have a family. I'm divorced, a two-time loser. If I fall, no one will miss me."

"Why are you interested in the tarot?"

"I'm still on the lookout. Thought maybe the tarot would help me pick better next time," she said. "We can take a ride and then go to my place and do practice readings on each other."

"I'm up for the ride."

I looked at my watch. A pleasant twenty minutes had passed and, she was right, I was breathing normally again. We agreed to bike around ten o'clock on Saturday morning.

We met at the top of the hill. Lorraine had a red racing bike with what looked to have about thirty gears. I had an old three-gear bike that my mom bought me when I was about twelve. Lorraine took off and was soon far ahead of me. To me, this proved we weren't compatible, and I thought this might be our only ride together. I was surprised when I got to the flat part. There was Lorraine waiting patiently for me. "That was fun. I watched you at the end. You never got close to falling off. It would be safe if you went faster."

"Maybe next time," I said. We rode slowly, side-by-side and talked.

We both loved to cook. I told her some of the tricks I'd learned to make the best pastries and cakes. "I'm single," she said. "It's dangerous to your figure to bake for yourself." She was more interested in the joys of slow cooking.

We talked about religion. I went to Catholic mass every week and she never set foot in a church. I like fashion and she wore what I rather snobbishly thought of as shabby. We didn't shop at the same stores. We didn't belong to any of the same organizations.

A pleasant fifteen minutes had passed, and we were back at our starting point. I was quite happy when she asked if I had time to go around again. This time she didn't ride down as fast, and I rode down faster. When we got to the slow part, we talked again. Both of us have black hair and a Mediterranean nose, her family was from southern France and mine were from Sicily. We talked about our friends but neither of us recognized any of the names the other mentioned.

Lorraine was the first to say, "I don't think we know a single person in common."

"Is that important?"

"It means we can gossip freely, and we can be sure it will never get back to us."

I remembered how I'd gossiped to one friend about how poorly my cousin was raising her daughter. My friend promised never to say anything to her. Two weeks later, my cousin stopped talking to me. My friend denied it, but she must have said something.

With Lorraine it would be completely safe to exchange private information. We began to gossip in earnest. "I have another cousin who is cheating on her husband," I said. "I like him much more than her. Do you think I should tell him? What would you do?"

"That's so common," Lorraine laughed. "How do you know he isn't cheating on her too? Why don't you ask him?"

"I could never do that. I'd be so embarrassed. Besides, it's very unlikely."

"You could ask. Most people love to talk."

"But then I'd know and have to do something."

Lorraine continued, "There's much worse than cheating. My neighbor Timo hits his wife, Jayne. Last week, I heard them yelling through the wall and then there was a loud thud. I knocked on their door and asked what happened. Timo said a box had fallen off the table. Jayne didn't leave the apartment all week, but I saw her on their balcony two days later with a shiner."

"How horrible."

"Nothing like some of the things I learned when I was a social worker."

She began to tell me stories of abuse, physical, emotional, sexual, and economic. She'd grown tired of fighting with some of her clients. She said that many had no desire or incentive to cooperate with her. She now works at a flower shop. Over many rides, she told me a lot of ugly but convincing tales. "Two of the hardest things are understanding and forgiveness," she said. "We're all capable of horrors. I always tried to make friends with my clients no matter what they did."

I began to wonder if all the stories Lorraine told me were true or if she was exaggerating to entertain, titillate, and impress me.

On about the tenth Saturday, she told me she was having a birthday party on Thursday and invited me to attend.

As we were approaching the steep hill, I asked her to tell me the worst thing any of the people, who would be at the party had done. "You're Catholic," she said. "I suppose to you, Yolda, who had five abortions, would be the worst."

"Five abortions? How is that possible?"

"Maybe she's had more. That's all she's told me about."

We raced down the hill, not together but much closer than previously. For me, it was both terrifying and exhilarating to go this fast. I was thinking and thinking about Yolda. When we got to the bottom, I said, "I don't approve but I understand. Maybe she thinks she's not emotionally capable of raising a child."

"I don't think she'd give a shit about your approval."

Then Lorraine told me about Paula who had drowned her two-year-old daughter in the tub. I thought she was making this up but later she showed me her scrapbook with newspaper clippings from years ago. There were articles and pictures. Paula was a short woman, with long blonde hair and her face looks like all the joy in the world had disappeared. She'd plead guilty and served fourteen years. "She'll be at the party. I'll introduce you."

I was the first to arrive and I helped Lorraine make a vodka punch. Lorraine's one bedroom apartment is on the ground floor at the end of the corridor. There was no apartment opposite to her and only one tiny studio that stuck out of the building to her right. There weren't apartments above the studio and Lorraine's was the only apartment that shared a wall with the studio. I could hear a TV on in the studio and the sound came right through the wall, almost as if it were in the room. "The old bat's going deaf," Lorraine said, "But I like her." Lorraine phoned her and the woman turned it down. She came to the party later. She used a walker.

It was a typical party. The music was low, there was a bit of subdued dancing, lots of drinking, Lorraine had made great food and there was lots of talking. I'm not sure how but she got more than forty people in at one time with people constantly leaving and arriving. Probably over a hundred people were at the party at one time or another.

The first people I talked to were Timo and Jayne. Was Lorraine's talk of Jayne's shiner true? They looked like they were getting along fine. I looked closer and Jayne's nose was partially collapsed, like a boxer. That could have many causes, but he might have hit her. Was it any of my business? Should I disapprove? I didn't.

I got a second glass of punch. Lorraine said, "Now's your chance," Lorraine pointed across the room with her eyes. "I'll introduce you to Paula Verbose. She uses her maiden name Thompson now."

I remembered that both last names were in the article. Paula looked twenty-five years older, but she was the one in the photos. She still looked depressed.

Lorraine introduced us and left us alone. We chatted about Lorraine for several minutes. Then Paula said, "You're staring at me. Why?"

"I'm not staring."

"Your eyes keep raking over me. Are you judging me?"

"I'm sorry," I said. "I often stare. I don't know anything about you. What did you do today?"

"I'm trying to find a job. It's been very hard."

"Yes, it can be. The recession's pretty bad."

"I've been out of work for a long time. It gets worse the longer you're out and the unemployment agencies are useless."

"I've heard that before. Did you ever think of starting your own business?"

"How could I? I'm broke. I'm staying with my brother and his wife wants me to leave. She'll force me out soon. Enough about me. What did you do today?"

I was embarrassed to talk about taking my daughter to her first piano lesson. I hadn't thought about how easy my life was and how hard life must be when you get out. I felt sorry for her. I told Paula that I'd be glad to speak to her again. She rolled her eyes as if doubting I was telling the truth.

When someone leaves their apartment, my husband has to re-paint it. It happens about twice a year. A few weeks later, one tenant left so I asked if he'd let Paula help paint. I told him she needed the money. He agreed. A month later, she got a full-time job working as a cashier in Key Food. We talked occasionally.

Years passed. We biked almost every week and gossiped frequently. Then two months ago, Lorraine lost her cheerfulness. I asked her why and she invited me to her apartment. As we entered the building, she said, "I mourn the dear old bat. I have two new neighbors in the studio." She opened her apartment door, and I backed up. High pitched yelps came from the next apartment. "It's perfectly safe. That dog, Mandy, is my second new neighbor in the studio."

She phoned the studio but there was no answer. A few minutes later, I checked my watch. A high piercing bark came about every fifteen seconds. I almost thought it would end when I heard another yelp. Over the next half hour, the pitch of the barks got a little deeper, but the volume and frequency continued the same. Forty minutes later, I said, "I've got to get out of here."

Lorraine told me that her new neighbor's job required her to switch from days to nights every other week. She spent the weekends at her boyfriends, leaving the dog behind and coming by to feed and walk her twice a day. When she wasn't there the barking could go for hours.

"God, that must be tough," I said.

I put my coat on and walked to the elevator. A short woman with a small dog came out of the studio next to Lorraine's. This dog had to be Mandy. She was small and had cute brown fur. Her tail was wagging furiously, and she seemed to pull the woman along. As we waited for the elevator, I asked the woman what kind of dog it was. "It's a Cairn Terrier," she said. Mandy barked at me a few times. On the elevator, Mandy rubbed up against my leg. I reached down and petted her. When we got out of the building, Mandy pulled the woman towards the park and started barking again. I walked in the other direction.

When I got home, I looked up Cairn Terriers. The article said they were frequent barkers and have a lot of energy and tend to become loud and destructive when bored. They're harder than most to train. Not a good choice for someone who lived in an apartment and was often absent.

The next time we biked, Mandy was the center of conversation. I didn't tell Lorraine that I'd seen the dog. Maybe I should have.

"Did you talk to your neighbor about the barking?" I asked.

"Constantly. She says I'm exaggerating. 'Mandy doesn't bark much. Besides, Mandy's my baby. If your baby cries a little, that's not a problem.'"

"Her baby? She leaves her alone for days. Mandy doesn't bark much. I've heard her. Don't the other neighbors complain?"

"It's only in my apartment that you hear it so loud," said Lorraine.

"Yes. I remember the layout."

"I've thought of moving but my apartment's rent controlled. I can't afford to," Lorraine said.

"What are you going to do?"

"Sometimes I think of capturing it, driving it to the country, and doing a clean execution," said Lorraine. "She never changed the lock when she moved in. I still have a key from the old bat. I can't believe I'm thinking about this."

"We all have fantasies. Sometimes I get tired of hearing my daughter play the piano and of my job and husband and I dream about going off to Hollywood to be discovered."

"You'd never do that," Lorrain said. "Yours is more of a fanciful mind vacation. Mine isn't. I almost wish I had a second job so I could be away from the barking most of the day and maybe I could deal with it at night. But I love having the extra time to do what I want."

"Mandy barks all night?" I asked.

"When she works nights. Would you hate me if I did it? I bet you'd never talk to me again."

I think it was the first time I directly lied to Lorraine but, at the time, it seemed like I was telling the truth. "I'd never get angry with you no matter what."

It went on for another month. I talked to Lorraine almost every day. I visited her apartment twice and the barking was intense.

A week later, we were riding. Lorraine looked rested and happy. I was afraid to ask but she volunteered. "On the first Monday of July, most everyone is out on vacation. She told me that she'd be out the whole day. I made Swedish meatballs and put two sleeping pills in them. That damned dog was soon asleep, and I took her out in a suitcase and drove to the country. I won't tell you the details, but that dog will never keep anyone awake again."

I smiled and was not the least bit clear about what I should say. I had helped Paula, who had murdered her daughter. Yolda had five abortions, and I chose not to judge her. Those cases were human life. This is only a dog. Why did it feel different?

I eat meat. How many chickens, pigs, and cows have I eaten, and I don't feel guilty? I told myself that my feelings towards Lorraine were irrational. There's no reason to let go of this friendship.

Suddenly, I snapped out of my thoughts and realized I was riding next to Lorraine. "What happened when your neighbor came home?" I asked.

"She started to wail, 'where's my baby?' She thinks the dog got out somehow. She's asked all the neighbors, and no one can tell her anything."

"At least it's over," was all I could think of saying.

The next Friday, Lorraine called to confirm we were biking the next day. I heard myself say, "I'm busy. I really can't." I did the same the next week.

Our family went away for a week to southwest New Hampshire. I turned off my cell phone. When we got back, I turned it on and there were three messages from Lorraine asking why I wasn't calling her back. I erased them. I let her next calls go through to voicemail and then erased them.

I don't want to see her, but I'm bound to do so, unless I give up biking in the park. Even if I'll give up biking, she might come over.

I knew she went swimming on Tuesday mornings at 10 a.m. I called at 10:15 a.m. and left her a message. "I can't explain it, but I am angry at you and even more angry with myself. I think we shouldn't see each other for a while. I'll call you when I'm ready." She called back but I didn't answer. The message went to my voicemail.

Cowardly, yes. It's been another month, and I still haven't gotten over it. Every time I think about Lorraine, I can't help but see her carrying the suitcase with Mandy drugged inside it. I've had dozens of different horrible visions of what happened next. I can't get rid of them. It's like getting a tiny pebble in your sneaker that you try over and over again to get out, but you never can. Every step reminds you that it's still there.

I know I must forgive her. I remember Lorraine saying, "Two of the hardest things are understanding and forgiveness." These feelings aren't good for me. Every morning, for the past week, I've vowed to call her that afternoon. Every afternoon, I can hear Mandy's cry and something inside me says "Not today."

Ambitious Alexander

"I've come up with another brilliant idea," yelled Alexander, who raised himself on his hind legs to speak to the seven other mosquitos feeding on the sweet nectar of a rose bush. None of them paid attention.

Maybe they didn't hear or understand, he thought. He screamed louder.

The only response was "What," from Erick, who'd been hatched from the same set of eggs.

The two had fed on the same flowers so often that they recognized each other and even gave what we might call a friendly buzz to each other. During the day, they slept under the same log and started their daily routine together. If any two mosquitos could be called friends, it was Alexander and Erick.

Their mom had bitten the great conqueror, Alexander the Great, of Macedonia. Somehow the insatiable, vainglorious ambition in his blood was passed on to our Alexander and, to a lesser, extent to Erick.

I AM going to impress them by learning to fly faster and higher than anyone, Alexander thought. He practiced for the next two nights. He could feel the air race by his body faster than he'd ever experienced before.

At twilight, he flew to an orchid, which had attracted many mosquitos. Alexander buzzed up, "Look at me, I fly the fastest."

If the other mosquitos had paid attention to Alexander, they would have noticed something unusual, through their great multi-lensed eyes. He was flying faster than any mosquito had ever flown before. But they weren't paying attention.

Alexander flew to a leaf and didn't move for a long time. Erick noticed Alexander wasn't feeding. He nudged Alexander in the direction of a flower. The two of them flew over to some lilies.

"Yum," was heard from Erick but Alexander was silent.

Alexander spent hours thinking about what to do next. Finally, it hit him. He'd fly upside down. He'd never seen a single mosquito do that.

The next day was devoted to trying to fly upside down. He flew in a straight line and gradually changed the angle of his wings, trying to make them perpendicular to the ground and then keep turning until he was upside down. Once he got past a certain angle, he lost control and plunged to the ground. His exoskeleton was so strong that he wasn't hurt.

Alexander had a new idea of how to fly upside down. He'd fly upward and curl back in a loop. After the curl, he'd be upside down. He failed the first seventeen times. On the thirtieth try, a female mosquito flew by. He flew his new barrel roll to impress her but now he was going in the opposite direction of the female. She continued flying straight, never noticing Alexander's success.

Flying upside down did not make Alexander famous. He had to think of something else that would impress the others. *I'm going to learn to silently hover in one place. Then humans won't be able to hear and swat us.*

With a great deal of practice, Alexander's wings still made a noise, but it was noticeably less than when he'd started. When he finally succeeded in learning almost-silent hovering, he noticed twelve feeding mosquitos on a flowering shrub. He hovered silently nearby. He shouted out, "I hover silently. I'm Alexander the Great." Only two mosquitos looked over and then looked away.

Later, Erick landed on a laurel flower and began to feed. Alexander was hovering silently. "This laurel is delicious," Erick called out. With the multiple lenses in his eyes, Erick saw a bird head straight towards Alexander. Erick sped towards Alexander and collided with him. They bounced in different directions. The bird missed Alexander.

"Why did you do that?" Alexander asked.

"To save your life," said Erick.

"I don't need the help of someone who is my inferior in every way. I can take care of myself."

Erick flew off in a huff.

Alexander kept pondering what would impress his fellow mosquitos. Feeding is the ultimate pleasure and necessity. *I'll be famous if I can learn to feed better.* His first idea was to find the best possible food, the fastest. No, everyone is trying to do that already. That's it. He'd feed on the rarest plants imaginable, the ones only he could find. Even four-leaf clovers were far too common. Having made a profound decision, Alexander began to implement it immediately.

Towards morning, Erick flew to where he and Alexander usually slept. Alexander wasn't there. Erick started searching for any mosquito flying faster than the others or hovering almost silently, but he couldn't see any. He couldn't find Alexander. Maybe he'd gone far away or been eaten.

Erick remembered what Alexander had told him about feeding off rare plants. He began looking for him in places where they didn't usually go. He asked a few other mosquitos to help him look for Alexander. All asked, "Who is Alexander?"

Erick began telling other mosquitos stories about Alexander's heroics. He was ignored. Slowly he became better at communicating. His constant talk of Alexander to the mosquitos under the log where they usually slept initiated the first real interest in Alexander. A few mosquitos even said they wanted to help look for Alexander, but they never did.

Erick kept looking for Alexander in more and more remote places. Finally, Erick found Alexander. He was emaciated, if one can use that word with a mosquito. He was sitting on a leaf, not moving. Erick called out, "Alexander, it's time for a good feeding. There's a flower only a short flight away."

"I don't feed on common plants," said Alexander.

"Are there any rare ones near here?" asked Erick. "You need a meal."

"There are a few but I've already had them. I need to find something completely new."

Alexander showed him some of the rare plants he'd already tried and said, "Find me something new that I've never had." Alexander then sat and waited.

Erick was happy. *Before I was just a common mosquito,* he thought. *Now I'm Alexander the Great's best friend and helper.*

Erick flew around but did not find any plant rarer than the ones Alexander had found. He was exhausted. He flew to a flowering shrub and fed. He had to rest after his meal. When he was revived, Erick flew to Alexander, who said, "I'm so weak, I can barely fly."

"That shrub is only a short distance. You can feed there."

"It's not rare. I'm not giving up now."

"You'll die."

"Leave me!" bellowed Alexander. "I will not hear your defeatist talk. I AM the most accomplished mosquito who ever lived."

"No one will remember you if you just die."

"I cannot give up my task."

Erick was so hungry that he flew off to feed. As he was flying, he saw a bird approach Alexander, dive and eat him. The greatest mosquito ever to live was now dead and gone.

Erick was despondent. He knew he'd never meet another mosquito like Alexander. He recalled all their moments together. Erick began visiting the places that attracted the most mosquitos. He called out, "I knew the best of mosquitos. He did wonders. His name was Alexander the Great. He was the fastest mosquito ever and he was the only one who could fly upside down and hover silently. He'd feed only on rare plants which are more delicious than any common plant."

The first five hundred mosquitos that heard Erick ignored him. Erick persisted. "What an interesting experience that must have been," said the five-hundredth and one.

A few days later, another mosquito said, "Alexander the Great was an artist."

Erick was so inspirational that many mosquitos began to speak of Alexander. These Alexander admirers had never actually seen or heard Alexander the Great. They didn't comprehend what Erick was talking about because

Erick never tried to show them how, for example, to fly upside down or hover silently. The stories told by the new Alexanderines became more and more wonderful over time. There were even a few stories about how Alexander killed the bird that tried to eat him. Millions of generations later, mosquitos still speak of Alexander the Great.

How did this author learn about Alexander? I am a mosquito magnet. They fly around my head and ankles probing for an opportunity to feed on my blood. Once, in the dead of night this infamous buzzing awakened me.

I called out "Tell me, why I shouldn't turn on the light and crush you?"

To my surprise, I heard a buzzing voice offering to tell me about the great mosquito Alexander the Great, if I would let her go free instead of swatting her. I agreed and heard this wonderful story which I've now conveyed to you.

Ambitious Alexander reminds me of the best of my fellow artists. I'm not saying you should listen and agree with everything an artist says or creates. We're far from perfect. Many of us, like Alexander, are egotistical and have an outsized opinion of ourselves. We're like blind people, who have heard that there is such a transcendental thing as light, which we have never seen and never will, but which we long to see and allow others to see. Our best efforts to craft this elusive light into something tangible are a pale imitation of the ideal we have imagined. We are like the person who desires to fly to the moon and must be content to jump three feet off the ground. "I'll make it to the moon next time," we cry out as we try again. In this new attempt we may reach three feet and a tenth of an inch or possibly this time only jump one foot and fracture our ankle when we hit the ground.

You might ask, why don't we stop? We, like Ambitious Alexander, have a secret power that enables us to continue this seemingly futile quest. What is this secret power? Can I, the reader, have that secret power? Certainly. But the secret power isn't what you expect or probably now want. An artist slowly and reluctantly loses the fear of what others call failure. The fear of appearing ridiculous. One can compare our artistic work to Edison's trials to invent the light bulb. "I have not failed. I have just found ten thousand ways that won't work." But that is a poor analogy. Edison knew he could invent a light bulb. Artists, being blind, do not know if we will ever succeed in expressing the miracle of light. We are like Sisyphus trying to roll a boulder up a steep hill, only to get it to the top and inevitably have it fall back to the bottom. Then we push it to the top again and it rolls back down. Endlessly. And we smile, at least inwardly, as we push the boulder. "I will make the tenth sketch today and this one will finally be perfect. Well, not quite perfect but I'll make it anyway." So, lets raise a glass filled with light, as a toast to Ambitious Alexander, the greatest mosquito ever to live. Alexander the Great.

It Is What It Is

"**Y**ou've got it all wrong," said Herbert.

He and his co-worker Robert were in their late-twenties and had worked together for two years. They had just sat down to lunch at a table in the Sakura Gardens Restaurant, which was two blocks from their office.

"You let your imagination control you," Herbert continued, "instead of being in touch with reality. I learned the secret of life that always works. I say to myself, 'it is what it is.'"

Their favorite waitress brought them their customary carafe of sake. Herbert poured each a cup.

"That's how you solve your problems?" asked Robert. "What does it even mean?"

Herbert smiled, pointing to his head and said, "It's the start of all wisdom. Tell me about any problem you have, and I'll tell you how this saying cures it."

"Haven't you noticed I look a bit dragged out?" asked Robert.

"I didn't think you'd want me to mention it."

Robert held up his cup, looked at it and twirled it a few times. He said, "My wife doesn't love me anymore."

"And how does that make you feel?"

"Like shit. I want her to love me."

"It's your imagination that's making your life difficult, not your so-called fact, which might not even be a fact," said Herbert. "Maybe she does love you."

Both men threw back their sake. Herbert poured them another.

"Nope," said Robert. "She changed the locks. No misunderstanding there. Spent the night at a hotel."

"The start of knowledge is to acknowledge that, 'it is what it is.'"

"What a dumb idea," said Robert frowning. "We can't just accept whatever happens to us."

"You have it wrong," said Herbert. "We can always say 'it is what it is.' and then start acting on this truth."

"You're contradicting yourself."

The waitress brought another carafe of sake. They both ordered miso soup. Herbert ordered salmon sushi and Robert rainbow sushi.

"I embody the saying it is what it is." said Herbert.

"You say it is what it is, but you don't approve of me disagreeing with that statement," said Robert. "You're trying to force me to change my point of view to yours."

"I can accept that you don't agree. It is what it is."

"So, you're not saying I'm making a mistake?" asked Robert.

Their soups arrived and they began to eat. They poured themselves another sake.

"It is what it is," said Herbert.

Robert shook his head, "You said that already."

"I did. I don't think you understand. Your thoughts are your thoughts."

"How does that apply to the fact my wife locked me out and I don't like it."

"Your wife's feelings are fine, and you need to accept that. It is what it is."

"And I suppose you'd say that my reaction to her throwing me out is also, it is what it is."

"Yes." said Herbert. "You have to start with that."

Their food arrived. They ordered a third carafe of sake.

"You seem to be saying nothing," said Robert. "What if I say that your philosophy is nuts?"

They put pickled ginger on their sushi and then dunked the pieces in wasabi mustard. The third carafe came. They ate and drank in silence.

"Man is that hot," said Robert.

Holding up his last piece of sushi, Herbert said, "It is what it is," in a whisper.

"And this sake?" asked Robert.

"It is what it is," said Herbert at full voice and this time with a huge smile on his face.

"I finally get it," said Robert, who for the first time smiled. "In the expression *it is what it is*, the word *it* occurs twice, and the word *occurs* twice. Those two words, *it* and *is,* are exactly the same."

"Has the sake gone to your head?" asked Herbert.

"I don't think so."

"You're confused," said Herbert. "It is what it is should be said as, *it is* with a pause *what* another pause *it is*. Got it?"

"I think so."

They were silent for a while.

Robert held up his cup of sake and said, "*It … it … is … is.*"

Herbert put his cup of sake down and said, "No. *It is … what … it is.*"

"How are we going to do any work this afternoon? asked Herbert. They both laughed.

"We will," was all Robert could say.

At the end of the day, Herbert asked Robert if he had anywhere to stay for the night. He didn't. Herbert offered his spare room. He noticed that his wife rolled her eyes when she saw Robert.

"It is what it is," he whispered to her. He noticed that she was shaking her head. There was little discussion at dinner or as they watched TV.

The next morning, as the two drove together to the train station, Robert said, "You know you're right and I was wrong. My feelings don't change reality. It is what it is."

"Let's just forget I ever said that," said Herbert.

"Why?"

"My wife told me that if I invite you back tonight, she's going to change the locks."

"How does that make you feel?" asked Robert

"Worse than shit."

"It is what it is," said Robert. "I finally get it."

"It's just a ridiculous saying," said Herbert

"No," said Robert. "*It is … what … it is.*"

They were silent during the rest of the ride in.

CHARITY

I wonder where she is, thinks Ryan. *She's always late.*

Ryan sits in the Spring Chinese Restaurant waiting. He treats Shela, a theatre director, to lunch there every month. *It's my charity,* he thinks. *The theatre's in a slump. I'm doing it to keep up her cheerfulness.* He sips Jasmine tea. The aroma makes him feel like he's in some place exotic and not in mid-town Manhattan.

He watches as the door opens and a woman, with dyed iridescent red hair using a cane, limps in. Each step looks painful but determined She says, "Sorry I'm late. Seems like I'm always late these days."

"It's nothing," says Ryan. "So glad you could make it."

"I always enjoy seeing you," she says. "Tell me about your projects."

"You first," says Ryan. "How's directing the theatre group for mature actor's going? What's their name again?"

"The Over the Hill Company. We're looking for the right piece. It's got to be over twenty years old and have lots of parts. They all want to get on stage."

"What plays did you look at?" Ryan asks.

"I had them read some Noel Coward, but they couldn't get the comedic timing down right."

"So wonderful to see you again," the waitress says to Shela. She gives them menus.

"Comedy is hard," agrees Ryan.

"Some say that tragedy is harder because it requires more emotional depth but making people laugh is …" Shela stops talking.

"How would you describe it?" asks Ryan as he pours her some tea.

Shela sips. "This is delicious. I just saw Jennifer, who was in your play."

"Did you say hello from me?" asks Ryan.

"Did you know she's thirty-five? I told her she really needs to push her career before it's too late."

"What did she say?"

"That there's plenty of time," says Shela. "No hurry. I tried to bite my tongue but couldn't."

"You do say what you think."

"There's only so much time to make a mark."

"How did she answer?" Ryan asks.

"If it's my fate, I'll accomplish my goals."

They order chicken with mixed vegetables and sweet and sour pork.

"I have the same thing to say to you," says Shela. "When are you going to start to concentrate?"

"I'm always concentrating," says Ryan.

"You're putting in the motions, yes, but really pushing your writing? No."

"What are you talking about? Ryan asks.

"When are you going to put emotional depth in your work? I read your first act. Deep emotion can be buried early in a play, but the seeds must be there from the start."

"I thought it was pretty good."

"Do you think your wife would be satisfied if you said you loved her pretty good? Or her cooking was pretty good? People don't go to the theatre to see pretty good."

The waitress brings their food.

"Thank you once again for lunch," says Shela as she spoons some sweet and sour pork into her plate. She takes a bite, "Love that combination of flavors. It's like comedy and tragedy combined perfectly."

"What were you saying about passion?" asks Ryan.

"You, especially you, need it for success. I want you to succeed. Maybe more than you do."

Always nagging me, thinks Ryan. "I've got passion."

"Not really You know I had a dance troupe when I was younger."

"I remember," Ryan says.

"I was commissioned to choreograph a modern dance," Shela says. "One of our dancers, Laura had a principal part. Her husband was jealous of her. Thought she was fooling around with another dancer. Anyway, at one rehearsal, he showed up with a gun looking for her. She was in the changing room. I told him she wasn't here, so he left. When she came out, I told her about her husband and asked if she wanted to leave. She said she wouldn't think of it. That's dedication."

"Did you call the police?"

"A pure waste of time," says Shela. "We had to go on in two days."

"What happened?"

"It was an artistic triumph."

"Is Laura famous now?" Ryan asks.

"That's not the point. She prioritized her craft. Wouldn't let anything stop her. That's what you need to do."

The lunch ends. Ryan pays. They have a hearty, heartfelt goodbye.

Two weeks later, Ryan texts Shela and they make a date for a week from then.

Three days later, a mutual friend calls Ryan. "Shela's dead," she says.

Ryan sucks in his breath and starts to pant, "How did she die?"

"She was found at home. Probably a heart attack."

"I was going to see her on Friday. Is there a service?"

"Nothing's been set up yet."

On Friday morning, Ryan feels nervous. Was he feeling depressed about the death? He remembers what a full, long, productive life Shela had. He doesn't feel any better. He goes to the Spring Chinese Restaurant and sits drinking Jasmine tea.

Ten minutes pass. The familiar waitress says "We've got a special today. Chicken with black mushrooms. Shela will love it."

"How do you know she'd love it?"

"She often told me how much she loves black mushrooms."

"That's good to know." The waitress left him. *Should I tell her?* Ryan wonders.

"She's really late," says the waitress five minutes later. "Wonder if something's wrong?"

Ryan wants to tell her what happened, but he can't find the words. He realizes that it was Shela who was supporting and helping him, not the other way around. He was the one receiving charity.

Ryan eats his chicken with black mushrooms. Later, it takes almost an hour to walk home. Thinking. *Who will push me now? Who will really care? I bet she'd have some great stories to tell me if she could come back now. I miss her so much.*

My Walk Home

"It's Sunday, 2:10 a.m. The weather is cool, and a few stars peak through the clouds. It would be a fine night except my hands burn, my back aches, and I'm exhausted. I just finished twelve hours of washing dishes at the Jubilant Restaurant and I want to get home to bed. I'd like to say to bed with my wife, but she left me when I was first convicted. I shout out, "Turn green, you damned walk signal! Turn Green. I'm tired of waiting. Change now!"

"Stop daydreaming!" said Mr. SummerCloud. "You're talking to yourself out loud again."

I'm standing waiting to cross Juniper Street, the first block I've got to cross to get home to my apartment. I've pressed the walk button eight times in the past ten minutes. The green light that tells cars to go has changed twelve times in that time but the Do Not Walk sign is still on. There are few cars this late at night, but I don't dare jaywalk against the Do Not Walk light because there are camera's everywhere recording everything I do and say. To most people, being caught jaywalking would go unpunished but officially it's a minor crime. I've agreed to obey every law, no matter how trivial, on penalty of death. "You're the one who suggested I promised to obey every law, didn't you, Mr. SummerCloud?"

"No, I urged you to take the prison sentence. Much safer."

"Yes, I remember now."

As I wait, my worry increases. I'm only allowed an hour to get home, and ten minutes have already passed. My mind starts to wander back to this afternoon's twelve-block walk to work. If I hadn't had to wait for the walk lights to turn on, before I got my ankle bracelet, four days ago, I could have easily walked the twelve blocks in under twenty minutes. My job starts at 2 p.m. Today, I started walking at 1:15 p.m. Forty-five minutes should have been plenty of time.

Right outside my building is the first intersection I needed to cross on my way to work. I kept pressing the walk button, but the green walk light never comes on. Finally, about seven minutes later, an older woman, pulling a wire-shopping cart, came up and pushed the walk button. Ten seconds later the green walk sign lit up. She started across and I followed maybe five seconds later. I wanted to cry out, "Please walk towards my restaurant or I'll get stuck again," but I didn't dare. She turned off to the right. That's the way to the food market.

I was then stuck waiting at the corner of Lilac Street. I'd pressed the walk button several times, but nothing happened. Do Not Walk is still illuminated. There was a purple lilac bush blooming there. When I grew up, my family had three lilac bushes that bloomed at the same time, purple, white, and red. Each had that entrancing lilac fragrance, but each scent was subtly different. I loved walking back and forth noticing the slight differences. I wondered if you could make three different perfumes from them.

Back then, I'd cut the lilac flowers for an ancient, wrinkled woman, Mrs. OldGold, who lived by herself. We'd often chat. She would talk about what she called "the good days before the Revolution." I knew I shouldn't listen, but she was so old and senile that I felt sorry for her. No one else noticed or talked to her. Before the revolution, her father owned a large farm that employed twenty-seven people. He was liquidated, of course. I repeated the revolution's three golden rules to her: "*The needs of the many outweigh the needs of the few or the one. The Party defines the needs of the many. Obey the Party and thrive; disobey and die.*" I told her, with what I then believed was loving honesty, that her father had put his needs over the needs of others, so his death was for the common good. I kept waiting for her to ask why my family had eleven servants and five cars. I had a good answer. My father was third in command of the Party during the revolution. He advanced the needs of the many and received his just rewards. Sometimes, when

I said it was good that her father was executed, she'd shed a few tears. I'd leave before she would start to cry. Someone might notice I was talking to an undesirable person.

"Stop daydreaming!" screamed Mr. SummerCloud. I looked at my watch and twelve more minutes had passed. I was going to be late for work again. I pushed the walk button again. Nothing. A teenager was walking towards this corner. I could almost hear her thoughts as she saw me: "Lazy bum. Maybe he's a criminal." She pushed the walk button and ten seconds later, the green walk sign lit up. I walked a little slower than she did so that I didn't frighten her. We walked across and then got to Crimson Street. She turned off to the left. I hit the walk button several times. Nothing. the Do Not Walk sign stayed illuminated the whole time.

The three stores on the corner of Crimson Street are long abandoned. A rancid odor oozes out of one store. It's so strong that the whole area stinks of corruption and death.

That sickly, rancid stench is what I remember most about my Time of Troubles. It was the brutal combination of sweat, dirt, and intense fear. It's not like the odor of exercise; it's more pungent, stronger, older, and more metallic. It smells like evil. Five of us were sitting blindfolded, on a platform with dunce caps on our heads. Our hands were tied behind our back. "Confess you traitors," yelled the mob. "Confess or we'll kill you." A few people threw stones at us. One hit me in the forehead. Blood dripped down to my mouth. I could taste it.

"I remember that time vividly," said Mr. SummerCloud. "Everyone had lost the ability to see their own cruelty and the capacity to question themselves. Did you think of yourself as a hero?"

"Yes, at first." I remembered how my questioner asked me to confess my crimes. I said proudly that I hadn't committed any crimes and that I was a hero for telling the truth. Then he explained to me the methods he used to get confessions. I heard screaming in the background.

He had me take off my shirt and raise my arms. He put a burning cigarette out in my left armpit. He lit another cigarette and said, "That was an appetizer. I won't put the cigarette out next time. I'll hold it there and puff. If you don't talk, I have many other, even better treats in mind. Have you ever heard someone scream when their balls are crushed? We can go on for days. A few people hold on for a week before they die or crack. Do we really need to continue?"

"No. I'll confess."

"You see how merciful I am. I gave you an easy choice. You should thank me."

I gave him a weak, "Thank you."

They sent me to a farm, as a slave, for rehabilitation. No pay, no rest, little food. "It was horrible," I told Mr. SummerCloud.

"I remember but you received two small blessings. You got in better shape, and you quit smoking."

Mr. SummerCloud was right. It would have been a hard, good life, except for the constant hunger and endless fear of re-arrest. I was lucky. When I got out, I found out that my father had been tortured and liquidated. I couldn't believe they'd liquidate such a great man. I thought of my old neighbor, Mrs. OldGold, and her father. How could I have told her that his liquidation was a good thing? I wanted to apologize to her, but she was long dead.

"Stop daydreaming!" yells Mr. SummerCloud, as I continue to wait. "Here comes a woman walking with a young girl. If you smile, she might help you." When she gets close to me, she frowns and steps to the side, to keep me at a distance. She presses the walk button. Fifteen seconds later, the walk sign is illuminated. I cross after her and try not to look in her direction, so she won't think I'm following her. They go two blocks in my direction and then turn off to the left.

I was stuck on Jewel Street. Mr. SummerCloud reminded me of my Diamond period. "Rehabilitation is more precious to a prisoner than a diamond is to a lover," he said.

After seven years on the farm, an official told me, "You've been appointed to head the Department of Sanitation in Meadow Lark City."

"Why me? Why now? I know nothing about sanitation."

"We just discovered that you are the child of a hero of the revolution. Why shouldn't you have a wonderful job? You've been working in the dirt. Sanitation is the perfect job for you."

I'll never forget my first day in charge. My every potential desire was anticipated and instantly fulfilled. If someone even thought I wanted something done, they'd do it. I found it both intoxicating and frightening. I asked Mr. SummerCloud, "What if they did what they only thought I wanted, and it turned out wrong? Would I be held accountable?"

"Stay calm," said Mr. SummerCloud. "At the current time, a Party official, who obeys his boss, doesn't need to worry about what his underlings do or think. Just do what you're told."

I looked at my watch and I was already late for work. The man who lives in the apartment next to mine walked up. I asked, "Would you please walk with me to my job?"

"How far is it?"

"Five blocks."

"You can walk that on your own. It will only take a few minutes."

"The walk sign never turns on when I push the button."

"You're crazy. It always works. Let me show you." He pressed the walk button and about twenty seconds later the green walk sign came on.

As we crossed the street, I said, "It works for you because you're not a political prisoner."

"Stop talking nonsense. There are no political prisoners. It's all in your imagination."

"I can show you my ankle bracelet. The walk buttons detect it and won't turn on for me."

"Stop being absurd." We walked straight toward my work, never waiting more than thirty seconds to cross the street.

"Told you it's easy," said my neighbor. "You only have one block to go."

"Have him watch you from a distance," suggested Mr. SummerCloud. "Then he'll see that the walk sign will never come on." I made this suggestion to my neighbor.

He rolled his eyes and said, "I don't have time to waste on such silliness."

"Please," I plead. "You think I'm crazy. It won't take you more than two minutes to find out if I'm telling the truth. Stand back and watch me hit the walk button."

"Not today," he said. He walked with me to the last cross walk, pressed the button and the walk sign came on. I heard him say under his breath. "What a nut."

When I got to the restaurant, I started washing dishes. In came my boss, Miss BrightSmile. She's only about twenty-five and until today had always greeted me with enthusiasm. "Late again?" she asked.

"The walk lights were against me."

"I wish you wouldn't make such a strange excuse. I'm afraid it's the third day in a row."

"I'll start for work even earlier tomorrow. I promise."

"Please do. I was asked if you came in late. I told them no, but they might come here and check for themselves."

"Thank you. It won't happen again." I went to wash the dishes, worried about the future and wondered who was checking up on me and why.

I enjoyed my job. No one bothered me. It was rewarding to know we serve good food to so many people. I enjoyed the smooth flow of work. The warmth of the water on my hands was so pleasantly sensual but by the end of the day, my skin wrinkled and my back ached.

I could smell the vegetables cooking with the sharp spices and hints of meats or fish to make our signature soups. "It smells so good," said Mr. SummerCloud. "I wish I could eat some."

"Now you're being absurd."

The succulent odors made me feel starved. I got a large bowl of soup for dinner plus I got two tea breaks with a pastry and tea. Every few hours, Miss BrightSmile checked to see that I was getting the dishes and pots done. There was never a problem with my work.

"Why don't you make nice to Miss BrightSmile?" asked SummerCloud. "She lives on this block and might invite you to stay with her and then you won't have to worry about being able to walk home."

"She'd never do that."

"She won't if you don't ask," said Mr. SummerCloud. I ignored him.

My twelve-hour shift ended at 2 a.m. *"Stop daydreaming!"* You must hurry. Its already 2:17 a.m.," Mr. SummerCloud reminded me. I was only allowed one hour to get home, and I'd been waiting for the walk sign for over ten minutes. Usually, late restaurant customers were going in my direction but tonight I hadn't seen another person out walking.

As we waited, Mr. SummerCloud asked me, "Tell me again why you publicly questioned the government's new sanitation policy. I never suggested that."

"My boss, the mayor, told me the policy would ruin the city and it was my duty to stop it by speaking up. He said he'd have my back. That's why I gave that speech and wrote to the newspapers."

"You never learn, do you? He was setting you up."

"But you told me to do what my boss requests."

"Not if he's doing something his boss disapproves of."

"How would I have known that?"

"I admit, I put you in a very difficult situation," said Mr. SummerCloud.

"Now you admit it. You never took any responsibility before."

"Let's say we both failed to anticipate the results."

I started to remember what happened next. It was all done so quickly. I was pushed into a car and taken to a small, windowless room to appear before a magistrate named Mrs. NeverLaughs.

As soon as we walked in, Mr. SummerCloud said to me, "She's a torturer."

She had an unlit cigarette in her mouth. "Slandering the State calls for the death penalty."

"Yes, Mrs. NeverLaughs," I said. "I agree. I know that but ..."

"Silence," she shouted. She calmly lit her cigarette, drew in a deep breath and blew smoke rings in my face. "I'll make you a generous offer. Plead guilty and you'll get the choice of either twenty-five years in prison or taking a special kind of probation. If you choose probation, you'll be released but you must obey even the smallest law on pain of death. We'll get you a job washing dishes."

Mr. SummerCloud whispered to me, "It reminds me of giving an old horse the choice between being sent to a glue factory or having to pull a cart all day long without food or water."

"I'm not a horse," I said out loud.

"Who said you're a horse?" demanded Mrs. NeverLaughs.

"The Party can't make money selling horses to make glue," said Mr. SummerCloud. "But they do execute criminals, harvest and sell their organs. Have you any idea what a heart, lungs, kidneys, eyes and liver go for? You're fifty years old. You might not survive twenty-five years in prison but at least you won't face execution."

"What laws could I possibly break washing dishes?" I asked Mr. SummerCloud.

"There are tens of thousands of laws," said Mr. SummerCloud. "Most you never even heard of. You're bound to break at least one."

"Stop talking to yourself and make up your mind," demanded Mrs. NeverLaughs.

"I can't face prison. I promise to obey every law."

It suddenly started raining and I didn't have an umbrella or jacket. I ducked into a store's doorway. It was the Madrigal Clothing store, my ex-wife's, JulySun's, favorite. Once, she took so long shopping here that I started walking around outside. She came out wearing a sheer blue blouse with gold trimming. She'd taken off her bra and her sweet nipples were poking through the silk. We rushed home as fast as we could go. It was heavenly.

"Stop daydreaming!" said Mr. SummerCloud. "She left you when you were arrested. She'll never come back now that you have a death sentence over your head."

I noticed that I still had only about thirty-five minutes before I broke my curfew. I couldn't just wait there. I had to try something. The green walk sign heading to my apartment was not illuminated but the one going parallel to this street was on. I could go there and then try the walk sign on that corner going towards my apartment. I ran and quickly pressed the walk button towards my apartment and waited. Nothing.

The city doesn't go on forever. The cameras and walk signs ended about a mile down this block at the edge of town. Every sign in the direction out of town showed walk. Of course they did. That way, I would be getting further from my apartment but at least I'd be moving. I started walking as fast as I could. I was huffing and puffing. Mr. SummerCloud was breathing normally. He is never tired.

Fifteen minutes later, I was beyond the edge of town where the walk signs and surveillance ended.

"I've done it! Mr. SummerCloud." I quickly walked down to the cross street my apartment is on. I just needed to walk up this block for half a mile and I'd be home. It was a fifteen-minute walk, and I had twenty minutes to do it.

Mr. SummerCloud tapped me on the shoulder and asked, "How naive are you? There will be don't walk signs all the way to your apartment and now we're back in the monitored area."

I got to the first corner, pressed the walk button but the walk sign didn't turn on. I tried the one going further away from my apartment. The green walk sign was on. I dare not go that way. I was trapped. I sat down on the concrete sidewalk, exhausted. Hours passed. Eventually, I saw a cab and at 7:58 a.m. I got to my apartment building.

The concierge asked me to give an account of my movements. "You left work at 2 a.m. and you took almost six hours to get here. You left the surveillance grid. Where were you and who did you talk to?"

I wanted to shout, "Leave me alone. Why do you care?" but instead I said, "The walk signs were malfunctioning last night. I couldn't jaywalk so I had to wait for a cab."

"The authorities will look into your explanation."

I was thinking of my promise to get to work on time. I knocked on my neighbor's door. When he opened it, I said, "It's Sunday. Do you think your son could walk me to work? I could pay him."

"That's very generous of you but he's in class all day."

"He doesn't have school on a Sunday. Are you refusing because I'm a political prisoner?"

"We both know there are no political prisoners."

"Please. It's supremely important to me. I must get to work on time."

"Absolutely not."

I went back to my apartment, set an alarm, lay down, and fell asleep. I dreamt I was walking on a narrow path through an impenetrable jungle. A lion appeared behind me and started walking slowly in my direction. Up the path, there was a deep pit with poisoned sharpened stakes on the bottom. I was paralyzed. Should I jump in the pit and hope I might make it out or hope that the lion would turn back?

I screamed and woke up. My door was open. Someone was shaking me. "Come with us," she demanded.

"Am I under arrest?"

"Of course not. Don't be foolish. Just come quietly."

I was blindfolded. We drove for about twenty minutes. When my blindfold was taken off, I was in a small, windowless room with two chairs. It smelled of sweat and urine. I sat across from a burly man, who introduced himself as Mr. LeadWeight. He had a pleasant, almost quiet, voice. He smelled intensely of ginger and honey.

He took out a pack of cigarettes and offered me one. I said, "I don't smoke." He lit one and said, "They calm me down and can be very useful. Your record says that one was put out in your armpit once."

I didn't answer.

He showed me photos of myself crossing the streets on my way home. Each one had the time on it. "It's clear you violated your curfew. That's a crime."

"But the walk signs were malfunctioning."

"We've checked. The walk signs are working exactly as designed."

"Designed to make me break the law?"

"What an incredibly absurd accusation. That's not the only thing. You deliberately walked out of the city to where there are no cameras. Leaving the city without permission is also a crime. Why did you do it? Who were you talking with?"

"I was trying to get home. The green walk signs would only let me go out of the city."

"Not another false excuse! You clearly broke many laws. To claim the walk signs malfunctioned, when they work perfectly, is a sign of insanity. I'm sorry but it's clear you violated your parole. As agreed to, by you, we're going to have to liquidate you. You should be thankful that we do it humanely by lethal injection."

"Stop daydreaming!" I shouted out.

Mr. LeadWeight replied, very calmly, almost in a whisper, "Neither of us is daydreaming."

"I want to appeal."

"I'm sorry. There's no time for that."

"Ask him for three wishes," suggested Mr. SummerCloud.

"He'll never agree," I said.

"Do you realize that you talk to yourself out loud?" asked Mr. LeadWeight.

I didn't answer. After a short pause, Mr. LeadWeight asked, "What won't I agree to?"

I was strangely calm and accepting of my fate, as if I had had a long, dreadfully painful, untreatable, terminal illness that had suddenly taken a sharp turn for the worse. My doctor assured me there was absolutely no hope but that I would have an easy, pain free death. "Can I make three last requests?"

"I'm a kind man. I'll grant them if they're reasonable."

"Tell me. Are you going to harvest my organs?"

"That charge is a slur against the state," said Mr. LeadWeight.

"When you grant last requests, you must tell the truth."

"Well then, yes. We'll harvest and sell your organs. Not to do so would be a crime against the many."

"Tell everyone who gets my body parts that I give them as a present."

"Agreed," said Mr. LeadWeight. "We'll say these parts were donated by a generous, anonymous donor."

"My second wish is that you drive me to my work and let me enjoy one last day there."

"Why?"

"One well spent day is more valuable than ten years of wasted time."

"You have to promise you won't tell anyone what's going to happen to you."

I promised. "My last wish is that you let me write up a history of my life and put the manuscript into a library. Maybe someone will learn from what I've gone through."

"We'll file what you write in the library of the Bay Leaf Facility for the Criminally Insane. The doctors there might find it useful. The public is not allowed in that library."

"Couldn't you put them in a library of my choosing?"

"That's not reasonable."

I had a great last workday. Mr. LeadWeight told them it was my birthday. We had a party when the restaurant closed. Miss BrightSmile hugged me and asked why I had never told them that I was such good friends with Mr. LeadWeight? I just smiled.

After work, I was driven to the Bay Leaf Facility for The Criminally Insane and given five hours to write. I couldn't think of what would be useful. Do I tell my story? Do I write philosophy? I just couldn't decide.

I asked Mr. SummerCloud what he would write.

"It depends..." he began to say.

I cut him off. "Yes, it depends. That's the key. I don't have much time, let me write about the three golden rules and what the phrase 'it depends' means to them."

I started writing. "Rule One reads: The needs of the many outweigh the needs of the few or the one. I say, it depends on what you mean. A better rule would be the needs of the many needs to be balanced with the needs of the few or the one."

As I wrote, I asked Mr. SummerCloud, "I wonder if anyone will learn anything from this?"

"To learn, one has to doubt that you already know the whole truth. Doubt is a rare, unpopular and sometimes a frightening virtue. Not one encouraged by the Party."

Mr. LeadWeight came into the room. "Times up," he said.

"I still have four hours left."

"You're writing nonsense. Why write anything more?" Mr. LeadWeight took the page, crumpled it into an ashtray, flicked his lighter, and burned it. We drove for about an hour and stopped at a large, guarded warehouse. Mr. LeadWeight showed the guards some papers. We went inside and he led me towards a door that said "Recycling."

I paused before I went through the door.

"What are you waiting for?" demanded Mr. LeadWeight.

I embraced Mr. SummerCloud and walked through the door alone. I believed that Mr. SummerCloud was the only person who will definitely miss me when I'm gone. The last thing I heard was Mr. LeadWeight saying, "That insane man just embraced the air."

ELEPHANTS INTERRUPTED

"It was a spaceship," yells Alexander. "Troy and I climbed in and met the crew. There were five of them."

There are nineteen guests, mostly friends and their kids at Troy's birthday party, packed into their tiny backyard. Her husband, Alexander, stands next to the grill, arguing with his best friend Jalen. Hickory smoke infused with the odor of baby back ribs fills the air. There are soy hot dogs grilling for Troy.

At last year's birthday party, Troy washed down the baby back ribs with pools of Chianti and a trip or two to the bathroom to smoke weed. Jalen and Alexander got into such a loud shouting match that a neighbor had called the police. The jarring sirens impelled Troy to undertake her oft-considered vow of sobriety. The two friends went fishing together the next day as if they'd never once argued.

At today's party, Jalen's and Alexander's argument continues. "That was the Numero Uno working, not a spaceship," shouts Jalen. "Best shit ever, wasn't it Troy?"

Troy takes a sip of her organic apple juice and thinks, *Sobriety is so hard and so over-rated.* Near the fence, her daughter and Jalen's son duel with Star Wars Ultimate Light Sabers.

"Alexander got a stepladder," Jalen continues, "and you two climbed onto your rock wall. Alexander said he'd wait there until a bird landed so he could talk to him."

"Sure. I was smoking but I was NOT hallucinating," bellows Alexander. "Tell him Troy."

"Well?" asks Jalen.

Troy frowns, "Why don't the two of you talk about something else? I've got to bring out the potato salad."

Alexander says, "Come on honey. Tell him. You got into the spaceship too."

"I don't like to remember that night," says Troy. "I vomited three times."

She hears her daughter shout out "I won," as Jalen's son falls to the ground.

"Come on sweetie," says Alexander. "Back me up here. We both climbed into the spaceship."

"I told you, I've got to get the potato salad."

"No problem," says Jalen. "First puncture his balloon. He sat on the wall to talk to some birds, and you joined him."

"I don't want to say," says Troy.

"I'll yell so loud the neighbors will come out if you don't say," says Alexander.

"Calm down," says Troy. "Everyone's listening." She glances over and her daughter and Jalen's son are fighting another duel.

"Tell us the truth and it will be over," says Jalen.

"Fine," says Troy. "I'll tell the truth. I sat on the wall and watched an endless line of gigantic pink elephants walk by. They had silver bells on their feet and tall, slim, blue men riding on their backs."

"No. It was a UFO," screams Alexander.

"Tell me more about these elephants," says Jalen.

Troy brings out the potato salad. She goes back inside to add a shot of vodka to her apple juice. *The hard part is to stop at one*, she thinks. *Or four.* Back outside, the argument continues. "Why doesn't anyone believe me?" shouts Alexander. "I'm telling the absolute truth. We got into a spaceship."

Troy sees her daughter fall to the ground; beat in the light saber duel. Her daughter jumps up, runs over, grabs Alexander's arm and yells, "Daddy, Daddy. Stop arguing. The food is burning."

"And One"

"It's a beautiful day here," said Mala, who was looking out the window from her home office in West Orange, New Jersey. She was the coordinator of a computer programming team for the Veztrone Corporation, an American company who several months ago began working with the Chinese giant Dragon's Fire to improve the software control system of drones. It was three minutes before their morning video call to review progress and problems.

Two others were on the call: a consultant programmer who lived in India, and Peter who lived in New York, the business leader, who officially controlled the work of the team. All the team members in the United States, except for one, were employees of Veztrone. The team members in India and one in New Jersey worked for an Indian consulting company.

"It's night here," answered one of the consultants in India.

"I wish we didn't make you work so late," said Peter. "You don't get to play with your kids. We get to work during the day."

"When I worked in India," countered Mala, "I worked at night too. It's just expected."

"I still think we're taking advantage of our Indian colleagues," quipped Peter. "It's a bit abusive."

Mala was angry. What gave Peter the right to criticize the company? Perhaps it was because he was nearing retirement age and didn't have to sweat through another thirty years of work.

Mala looked down to see that most of the team had joined the call. She was happy that David Thunder, the Vice President of Software Development and Security, wasn't there because he'd be angered by Peter's remarks. David continually pushed to finish projects in the shortest possible time. The team had committed to an ambitious schedule, but he had forced them to add what he called "optional additional work," which the team believed to be impossible to accomplish.

Mala said, "Let's start. Everyone who isn't speaking should go on mute."

One programmer began, "Issue 3454 is having problems with heap space..." Everyone listened intently except for Peter, whose mind tended to wander when going over the technical minutia of each ticket. He was thinking back to the Lakers victory in the National Basketball Association finals. Boy was the King of Basketball, LeBron James, great.

As the reports continued, a cell phone could be heard in the background. Aynur, the new intern, was the only person not on mute. She answered and put the call on speakerphone.

A woman's voice said, "Erkin wants to make sure you don't tell a single person about the difficulties he's had. You don't want him to get into trouble again, do you?"

Mala should have told Aynur that she wasn't on mute, but the mention of trouble had piqued her curiosity. She wanted to hear the details.

"I'd never say anything," said Anyur.

"We've intercepted a text message you sent. You said Erkin is in a re-education camp. You mentioned forced labor. We train people for new jobs. Everyone in Xinjiang is happy."

"I won't say a word. I promise."

"You also said Meryem had been gang raped by the guards. If you repeat that lie something terrible might happen."

"Why are you saying this to me?"

"Your company is important for our plans. We're watching you." Suddenly, the conversation ended. Mala noticed that Aynur had gone on mute. After the meeting, even though everyone was shocked, no one told Aynur they'd heard her private call.

Aynur's head was pounding. She tried to work but she made no progress. She knew she'd hit mute at some point but had the team heard almost the entire call? What was she to do? She thought of speaking to Jiniya, her closest friend on the team, but could she be trusted? Aynur didn't know, so she decided to keep quiet.

Until two weeks ago, Aynur's relatives hadn't heard from Erkin or Meryem for the past two years. Long ago, the three of them had perfected a secret language using one common word to mean something different. Erkin had gotten Aynur a secret message. He was out but had got "a face shot with happy grief." Aynur remembered when they'd invented that particular phrase. They had pretended they'd been in a car crash and almost died and described it using these same words. So Erkin had almost died. Meryem had told her that she'd suffered an "eel attack." Aynur shuddered.

Jiniya and Peter were the only members of the team who comprehended what they'd heard.

Aynur was in college with Jiniya's daughter. She had stayed at Jiniya's house during a number of vacations. Anyur was vivacious and fun loving but seemed to be fighting to hide some deeply hidden fear, which she never talked about. Now, Jiniya understood Aynur's fear.

Aynur was a computer science major and having real work experience would help her get a permanent job. Jiniya sponsored Aynur for an intern position. Peter gladly seconded the recommendation. He'd worked with Jiniya for twelve years and they enjoyed chatting about history, culture, and cooking. There's nothing like working through emergencies to bring people together and they'd been on scores of crises calls together. Plus, they both were slowly losing sight in one eye, Jiniya's the left and Peter the right. Jiniya teased that "eventually, it will take both of us to be able to walk down the hall without hitting the wall." Peter laughed but the possibility of going blind terrified him.

Jiniya thought about Aynur's call. She couldn't do anything immediately, so she went back to writing software to control drones. People will use these drones to lighten their work, she said to herself as she drifted back to work. What should she do for Aynur? She had no idea.

Peter knew what the call was about because he was a member of Pardon International, which worked to promote human rights around the world. He'd written over five thousand letters to officials in many countries including almost a thousand to China. To his surprise, a few officials had written back. The only letter that made sense to him was from an official who said that in his part of the world, if someone said they would kill you, they would definitely try to do so, and the person Peter was writing about had publicly threatened to kill people.

I can understand locking up a few people, thought Peter, but in Xinjiang, China there's mass imprisonment of millions, slave labor, rapes, forced sterilizations, and forced abortions. Over the past forty years, I've watched the human rights situation in China get worse and worse.

Several countries had recently declared that the government's treatment of the Uyghurs is genocide, the attempted destruction of a whole people. Peter was sure people would now take the situation seriously. Peter knew the Pardon investigator who studied this situation and asked if he could be informed if she heard any news of Erkin or Meryem.

Should Peter contact Aynur? She'd only been on this team for a week. They barely knew each other. Maybe he shouldn't interfere. Maybe he could get his company to do something to protest the genocide making sure not to mention what he'd just heard.

Veztrone's CEO had declared that respect for the rights of all people was the fundamental principle for Veztrone. He had a blog. Peter thought that perhaps, he should write about the genocide in his blog. No, that might put the CEO in a difficult position since the company was in a joint venture with China. Better to send him an email and let him decide to take the needed steps.

Peter wrote a note to the CEO saying the *Wall Street Journal* had an article about corporations responding to the declaration of genocide and asking if he had read it and then asking what Veztrone intended to do about the situation. Peter had the email ready to send but he wondered if he might be doing more harm than good. He also wondered if he was endangering his job and his safety. The Chinese Communist Party viciously retaliated against any person, company or nation who criticized them. The Chinese security law, which mandated life imprisonment for criticism of the party, had in 2020 been expanded to now apply to every single person on earth, whether living in China or not. If he was ever captured by the Chinese, he could go to jail for life.

One coach in the National Basketball Association had protested China's crushing peaceful protests in Hong Kong and had been made to take down the tweet or be fired. Peter wondered if even LeBron James, the King of Basketball, had the freedom to criticize the Communist Party. Nope. Even LeBron had lost his freedom to speak about Chinese abuse. *I'm nobody. I could easily lose my job.* He let the email go to the draft folder and started working on another project.

Later that day, Peter saw the email in the draft folder. He felt fear, noticed his heart was pounding. He said to himself, *yes, I'm afraid to send this. Yes, I could lose my job. What's the old advice? Feel the fear and do it anyway?* He pressed send.

The next day, the CEO wrote back that the company was waiting for the State Department to issue a finding that this was indeed genocide. Peter relaxed. There wasn't anything further he needed to do.

The work at Veztrone continued as it had done before the call. A few days later, David Thunder, the VP of Software Development and Security joined the call.

The team reported that although they'd have to work very hard, they'd make their committed goals.

David replied, "Making those goals is easy. I'm sure you will get the optional extra work done too."

"That's going to be very difficult to do," said Mala. "The committed work is already more than a full boat."

"You were willing to list the work as optional at the start. You must have believed you could do it."

One consultant thought, *we only agreed to list the optional work because you insisted* but he said nothing because as a consultant his opinion meant nothing. He didn't feel comfortable speaking up. He'd had scores of similar conversations with the David, and he always lost, often being verbally humiliated in the process.

"We'd like to do the optional work," said Jiniya, "but it looks like we can't."

"I can't understand why such a talented team can't get all their work done," said David. "Convince me why you can't."

I'm supposed to be in charge of this group and make that decision, bellowed Peter's mind. *David doesn't care if he forces them all to work around the clock without any overtime pay.*

"The team doesn't have time to add the extra work," said Peter. He noticed a sharp tone of anger in his voice but continued, "The quality of the other work will suffer."

"I'm the VP of Software Development and I don't see that," said David. "You don't do any programming work.

I'd need to hear that from the developers. They're doing the work."

This is an abuse of power, screamed Peter's mind. His neck was so stiff; he had to twirl his head around to loosen his neck muscles. Should he challenge David again? What do I have to lose? Well actually quite a lot. I need to work another five years, and David completely dominates upper management. They'd as likely disagree with him, as they'd refuse a million-dollar bonus. Then Peter thought of Aynur's situation. That really was a serious problem but that could wait, he'd have to say something here. "We should finish the promised work before we take on new optional work."

After three more exchanges, David each time insisting that he hadn't heard a single valid argument against doing the extra work, the team agreed to include the optional work. Another week passed. The team, especially the consultants, worked even more unpaid overtime.

At each morning meeting, Aynur was silent and sullen. Jiniya asked her daughter to invite Aynur over to her house, but she refused to come. She was unresponsive when Jiniya tried to talk to her.

There was another article in the *Wall Street Journal* that employees at a major software company had written comments on the company's blog about the Xinjiang genocide. Peter decided to write to the CEO again, telling him about the new article.

Before he did so, Peter wanted to compare the scale of the abuses in China to other historical abuses. He decided to look at the number of slaves in the United States in 1860, Jews murdered in the Holocaust, people killed in World War II, and those killed by the Chinese Communist Party.

There were around four million slaves in 1860, thirteen million people murdered in the Holocaust, and eighty million people, including civilians, killed in World War II.

How many had died as a result of the actions of the Chinese Communist Party? Estimates of those murdered or starved by Mao were well above forty million. The regime had also forced women to abort their babies. Was that murder? That was a harder question to answer but Peter always used himself as a reference point. Suppose I meet a pregnant woman on the street and forced her to have an abortion. Would I consider I'd done murder? Definitely. So that too must count as murder. There had been over three hundred thirty million forced abortions in China.

In total, the Chinese Communist Party had murdered over three hundred seventy million people. This number was beyond Peter's wildest imagination. It couldn't be true. Peter checked other sources. Yes, it was accurate. How could it be that no one talked about it?

Peter was physically sick. When he thought of bringing these facts to other people's attention, he felt as embarrassed as he was in his dreams, when he was giving a talk at work and looked down to see that he was naked. Why was he embarrassed? He didn't know. He checked his figures a third time. He wasn't making any of this up. Three hundred seventy million murders. That is greater than the total number of people living in the United States and Canada. He imagined traveling both countries and seeing every single person slaughtered and rotting on the roadside.

Peter graphed the statistics on a chart. He had to enlarge the chart to a maximum to even be able to see the sliver for the number of slaves or those murdered in the Holocaust. The Chinese Communist party had committed more than four World War IIs against their own people. I bet no one has any idea of the magnitude. I sure didn't. If they killed that many of their own people, would they hesitate for a second to kill everyone in the United States, India, or Europe. Extremely doubtful. A quote from Peter's favorite fictional detective, Hercule Poirot, ran through his mind, "With a murderer, it never ends."

Am I prejudiced, Peter wondered? I've worked to stop human rights abuses on every continent. It can't all be prejudice. People do horrible things to each other all over the world. Would people think me mad if I use these numbers? Maybe. Does it matter? No.

Peter went to the bathroom and vomited. He continued to retch even when nothing further came up. He got up and tried to wash the taste out of his mouth. It wouldn't leave. Nor would his anguished thoughts that, as a human being, he had this same potential to do sickening, vile deeds.

Maybe the only thing that can prevent such horror is to know, beyond a doubt, that all humans have the ability to kill burned into their DNA. Only an unflagging respect for other's lives and views could prevent it.

The problem wasn't the Chinese people, but a monstrous belief system forced on them. What can be done about the numerous belief systems, like communism, that believed that terrorizing and murdering one's enemies was not only necessary but noble? Peter had no idea. He was exhausted. He lay down on the bathroom floor and fell asleep.

When he woke, he went to his computer, wrote an email to the CEO about the employees who had written blog entries about genocide and asked what Veztrone was going to do. He asked why are we helping the Chinese Communist Party? He was more afraid than the first time he'd written an email but again he decided to ignore the fear. He sent the email.

Two days later, the CEO replied mentioning no actions being taken by Veztrone and saying that the company had absolutely no relationship with the Chinese Communist Party.

When Peter read this, he thought, this man is either naïve or a liar. No, I'm wrong to call him a liar. That's just a trap. It's so easy to say and think badly of others. Surely, the CEO knows there are no independent entities in Communist China. Every institution, company, club, university, church, sports team, organization, every person not in prison, is dominated by the Party, subsumed by the security apparatus. By law, every organization had to aid and obey the party. No CEO could be ignorant of that. Could they?

Peter remembered the mandatory course on modern slavery given to all employees of Veztrone. Every person in Communist China fits the definition of a slave. They can be jailed, tortured, killed, have their wealth confiscated at the will of the party. Peter had followed hundreds of cases over decades. To be accused is to be convicted. Secret courts, torture, disappearances. Peter thought of the old saying that a person is unlikely to see what he's paid not to see. The CEO was paid not to see these horrors and this risk or, if he did see them, to lie about it.

The Chinese Communist Party had just crushed freedom in Hong Kong, despite having signed a treaty saying they'd respect Hong Kong's democratic institutions. They vowed to enslave the twenty-five million people of Taiwan. Peter eyes swept over their claims on his office wall map. They claimed to own vast expanses of ocean outright. A United Nation's court declared these claims to be nonsense, but China was actively extending the military enforcement of their claims. In the past year, they'd attacked the Philippines and India and intimidated countries, companies and individuals around the world.

No, I'm being absurd, thought Peter but then he knew this wasn't true. Once you've read the original Communist

Party documents, you can't unread them. The Chinese President Xi, who recently declared himself dictator for life, had written about his plans. He vowed that every knee on earth would bend to his will by 2049, the hundredth anniversary of the revolution. Peter thought of what that official had written him. In his part of the world, if someone threatened to kill you, they meant every word of it. President Xi meant every word of his threats. It can't be Peter thought. I'm exaggerating. No. Three hundred seventy million murders is not an exaggeration.

Monday arrived. David called Mala to tell her that Aynur no longer worked at Veztrone. He wouldn't give her any more information, but Mala believed that Aynur had been fired.

Jiniya asked Aynur to come over to her house for a cup of tea. Aynur refused. Jiniya drove to Aynur's apartment and knocked on the door, but no one answered. She knew Aynur was there. Jiniya waited two minutes and knocked again. Jiniya shouted, as loudly as she could, "If I must, I can stay here all day. Let me in." A woman in another apartment popped her head out the window and shouted, "You're shouting louder than a tiger, go away." Jiniya shouted again, "Aynur, I know you're in there. Let me in."

Aynur opened the door. To Jiniya, she looked like someone who had almost drowned on a hurricane-flooded street.

"Why were you fired?" asked Jiniya.

Anyur slowly began to speak, "I violated the security policy."

Jiniya shook her head. "You're an intern. You didn't have access to anything important."

"I told someone my password."

"You what?"

"David said he needed to check to see if I had access to the unload dataset and asked me to give him my password. I said we're not supposed to do that. He said, '*Do you know who I am? I'm the Vice President of Software Development and Security. I have the authority to demand your password. Now give it to me or face the consequences.*' So, I did. About fifteen minutes later, I got a visit from security saying I was terminated. I was escorted out of the building."

"Bastard. You should sue."

"I'd never win. Besides …"

Jiniya understood.

A week later, at 6 a.m., Pardon International's investigator called Peter to tell him that Erkin had been found dead with the marks of torture on him. "They bind people's hands and feet to steel chairs, and then begin to use fire, electric shocks, and beatings. Not sure which were used on Erkin, but his body was a mess."

What to do? It was too late to help Erkin. Peter felt powerless and depressed.

He started to make breakfast but burned his eggs. Ideas surged like raging floodwaters, almost drowning him. The

Chinese Consulate is in Manhattan. We could organize a protest in front, invite the press, have people chained to chairs and demonstrate torture techniques. That might work. Maybe we could hand out leaflets every day during business hours.

And what of those nuns who bought one share of stock and entered a resolution at the annual shareholder's meeting. That was an idea.

I've loved working at Veztrone, thought Peter, but I can't help them to enslave mankind. I have to get my resume ready.

Peter was sitting in his kitchen when it was time for the daily meeting. His mind was still consumed by thought. He didn't join the meeting. It was the first morning meeting he'd ever missed. After the meeting, Mala called Peter's work number, but he didn't answer.

Later that morning, Jiniya called Peter on his cell phone. They went on facetime. Jiniya asked, "Are you OK?"

"I'm fine. Just thinking."

"What about?"

"A number," said Peter.

"What number?"

"Three hundred seventy million."

"What a strange number to think about."

With tears falling down his cheek, Peter added, "And one."

"Oh no."

Peter told Jiniya all he knew about Erkin.

"Is there nothing anyone can do?" asked Jiniya.

"I called a few people I know in Pardon International to see if they'd help set up a demonstration. It's possible. And shareholders can offer resolutions at the shareholder meeting. I don't know any of the details yet."

"Did you own a share?"

"Not yet," said Peter.

"I'll buy one too. I'll get an order page up."

"Me too. Let's hit enter at the same time. Ready? Go."

They were both silent for a second.

"I got a confirmation," Peter said.

"Me too," said Jiniya. "When's the meeting."

"Three months. Who knows if we can get a resolution in. We now have two shareholders who will show up to demand action. Maybe we can get hundreds more. A share is only $63.22."

"Aren't you afraid of making it worse for Anyur?" she asked.

"Three hundred and seventy million and one murdered. It's already worse. Time to stop being afraid." said Peter.

"Yes. It's time to stop being afraid. But to tell you the truth, I am."

"I am too," said Peter "but I'm getting used to that."

THE PERSONAL STATEMENT

Sam Iam and Elizabeth Stonington, two college seniors majoring in mathematics, were sitting in the kitchen of Sam's apartment, working on their homework. In the background, they could hear his son and daughter, in the living room, arguing over which game to play. His wife was out food shopping.

"Is it possible to train your kids to be a little less noisy?" asked Elizabeth, who was twenty-one and single.

Sam, who was thirty-one and had joined the marines to see the world when he was eighteen, laughed. "Can you count to infinity?"

"Of course not," replied Elizabeth.

"You can't make them to be less noisy either. You get used to it. They help me to concentrate."

"I'm not sure their helping me."

"Let's start with our Algebraic Topology course," said Sam. "I can't figure out question number three."

"I think the equation Y equals sine of one over X where X has a limit going to zero works," said Elizabeth.

"There's a discontinuity there," said Sam "but wow, I'd love to see that function graphed."

"Remember, we have to finish applying to our preferred graduate school," said Elizabeth. "I haven't even started on my personal statement yet."

"Me either. Let's look up the requirement."

Elizabeth read, *Requirement: A Personal Statement that says why you want to attend our university, what you hope to accomplish, and how you will use your degree to help make the study of mathematics more diverse and equitable.*

"The first two are easy," said Sam. They have the best program, and we want to get our doctorates. It's the third answer they're probably most interested in."

"You're right," said Elizabeth, "we have to convince them we'll help those who don't have access to mathematical study."

"Ninety-seven percent of students would probably drop math altogether if they could," said Sam.

"That's an exaggeration," chuckled Elizabeth. "It can't be more than ninety-five percent."

Sam laughed. "Are we supposed handcuff them and force them to study math?"

"You can't write that," said Elizabeth. "You have to convince the university you'll dedicate yourself to diversity and equity."

"How does a personal statement guarantee that?"

"It's not a guarantee," said Elizabeth, "but the statement can show you're sincere."

"Sort of like meeting a girl at a bar and saying you'll marry her next year if she'll have sex with you tonight?"

"Yeah, sort of like that", agreed Elizabeth

"Suppose I say I'm very sincere and the next person says, I'm very, very sincere and the third person says, I'm very, very, very sincere. This last person gets the gig, right?" asked Sam.

"That's probably how it works," agreed Elizabeth. "But you're being a bit cynical here. There aren't as many women studying mathematics and part of the reason is accepted gender roles. I'd like to help other women."

"I buy your sincerity," said Sam, "because I know you. But if I just read something you wrote, I'd think you might be faking it. You know the old statement, 'Don't trust those who speak much of their honesty.'"

"We have the same grade point average, so we probably have about the same chance of getting in. I'm going to write a personal statement to blow their socks off with my sincerity to help others."

"I'm going to have no part in that BS. I'm going to take an original approach.

"What are you going to do?" asked Elizabeth.

"Haven't figured that out yet."

"I bet I get accepted over you."

"Time will tell," said Sam. His two kids were no longer arguing. He went to make sure they weren't in any real trouble. Sam's wife came home and said that Sam had to drive their son to basketball practice.

"Let's open our acceptance decision letters from the university together," suggested Elizabeth.

"Sure," said Sam. Sam's son yelled, "Hurry dad. We're late." Elizabeth, Sam, and his son left.

Two months later, Paul, the Faculty Advisor for the Mathematics Doctorate Program and Linda, from the Admissions Office were going over the final two applications."

"We've only got one spot left and two perfectly balance applicants, Elizabeth and Sam," said Paul. "We should read their personal statements for a second time."

"I don't need to read them a second time," said Linda. "It's clear that we should accept Elizabeth and reject Sam."

"Let's not be hasty. Read me Elizabeth's again."

"Here it is," Linda began reading, *I am totally dedicated to using mathematics to solve the pressing problems of our day. Because I'm a woman, some people have suggested I become a high school teacher instead of pursuing my doctorate. This attitude needs to be fought. This assumption and the lack of availability make it difficult for a woman or a minority to pursue this career. I am supremely, sincerely, specially dedicated to using my supreme savvy to bring mathematics education to less served communities who absolutely crave this opportunity.*

There is not one applicant in a hundred as dedicated to this noble task as I am.

"That inspires my heart," said Linda. "Sam's is crap."

"Read it out anyway," said Paul. "I forgot exactly what it says."

"Here goes," said Linda. *What are ten thousand personal statements thrown into a bonfire? Don't ignore my question. Answer me! I'll put the answer on the next page, so you have time to think.*

"Not your average personal statement," chuckled Paul. "Reminds me of an old joke about lawyers." Linda scrolled to the next page and continued reading.

Ten thousand personal statements in a bonfire are ten billion too few! Burn them all!

Paul started to cackle and held his hand over his mouth to try to stop himself from laughing. Linda continued reading.

Mathematics demands absolute honesty. Demanding promises of future conduct is blackmail and should never be required. It only encourages lies. Please tab to the next page.

"He does have a point," said Paul.

"Accusing us of using blackmail," said Linda. "How dare he! That disqualifies him."

"It continues," said Paul. *I will tell anyone who will listen about the glories of mathematics. Of fractal worlds of infinite beauty and complexity. Of the beauty of the weather equation that is so sensitive to change that the beating of a bird's wings in California can change next week's weather in New York. Of one infinity which is infinitely larger than another. Of numbers so immense that if we used every atom in the universe, we still couldn't write them down. Mathematics is infinitely beautiful and studying it will enhance any individual. The numbers zero to nine do not discriminate. Neither will I. I will help any person who asks me for my help.*

"We asked how he'd help disadvantaged communities," said Linda. "He says he won't. That statement disqualifies him."

"I don't know," said Paul. "What's the biggest asset in solving tough mathematical problems?"

"Hard work and discipline," said Linda. "If the person craves helping society, they'll tough it out."

"Hard work's important but it's creativity and joy that makes the difference. Looking at a problem from a different angle and smiling when you fail. Which of these two statements shows more creativity and joy?" asked Paul.

"I'm still going with Elizabeth," said Linda.

"I'm with Sam. Besides, he'll excite people about mathematics. That will draw people who never thought of studying math. And he sounds like a hoot. I'd love to have him in one of my courses."

"You're nuts," said Linda.

"I plead guilty," agreed Paul. "Let's compromise and accept them both."

"There isn't room."

"Maybe some of the others won't come here," said Paul. "Let's give Sam a chance."

"What if other administrators read his statement and criticize us for accepting him? asked Linda.

"We'll tell them that they can make the tough admission decisions next year," said Paul.

"That'll shut them up," said Linda. "Who would want to do this job? I give in. We'll accept them both."

Two weeks later, Sam and Elizabeth were in Sam's kitchen. Sam's wife and kids were out. Sam was making a cake for after dinner.

"We promised to open our application answer letters together," said Elizabeth. "I've got mine."

Sam went to his bedroom and came back with his unopened envelope.

"You first," said Sam.

Elizabeth opened her envelope and started to jump up and down. "I got in and got a fellowship too."

Sam looked at his envelope and shook it. "It doesn't make any noise," he said.

"Don't be stupid," said Elizabeth. "Go ahead. I'm sure you got in too."

"I'm not so sure." Sam opened his envelope and said, "Wow. I got a fellowship too."

"You must have sent them an ordinary personal statement."

"Like hell I did," said Sam.

"What did yours say?" asked Elizabeth.

"Forget it. We're in."

Sam went back to mixing the cake, adding cinnamon.

"Now comes the even harder part," said Elizabeth, "our homework."

"Let's start with the Laplace Transformation," Sam said. "It's baffling."

"Yeah," agreed Linda. "Now I can tell the truth. At least ninety-nine percent of the population would avoid this equation."

She looked over at Sam and asked, "You're adding peanut butter to your banana cake?"

"Just a spoonful. Adds some zest."

Sam put the cake in the oven. "Stay for dinner?"

"I'd rather get a drink later this week," said Elizabeth.

Sam's wife returned with their kids. "Did you open your acceptance replies yet?" she asked.

Elizabeth shouted, "We both got in and got fellowships."

"That's so wonderful," Sam's wife said. There was loud shouting in the living room. Sam went to see what was happening.

"I have to thank you," said Sam's wife. "He'd never have made it without you."

"Are you kidding?" asked Elizabeth. "I'd have never gotten through if we hadn't done our homework together.

"Stay for dinner and celebrate with us."

Elizabeth stood there, not knowing what to say. Finally, she said, "Why not? The kids can't be harder to deal with than a Laplace Transformation."

"I wouldn't count on that," said Sam's wife, "but I wouldn't trade them for a hundred tons of gold."

When she tasted the cake, Elizabeth said, "This cake couldn't have been made by anyone but Sam."

Sam's daughter shouted, "Last week, I made a cake with anchovies."

"That was the best damned cake ever made," said Sam.

Elizabeth started to laugh, soon joined by the rest of the table.

A Frown Lit by Road Light

"You've read the brochure we sent you?" asked a practitioner from Antigua, over the phone. Harvey didn't answer. The distant, disembodied voice continued, "I guarantee we can cure your wife in twenty-one days. We've just lowered the fees so there's no reason to refuse."

Harvey shook his head back and forth, thinking *not again*. While the call dragged on, his mind began to wander over the past several years. So much had happened. He couldn't remember all the events, but the beginnings and the highlights were seared into his memory.

The first illness wasn't concerning. Harvey lived with Isolde, twenty-three, his wife of a year, in a one-bedroom basement apartment in Cherry Hill, New Jersey. It was an illegal apartment on a tree-lined street, which somewhat lowered its price. Both worked. Isolde was in good health. Yes, she'd had three colds and two fevers over the past year, which was more than most people, but that wasn't alarming.

On a sunny Thursday morning, Isolde's temperature was 103 (39.4 C). She stayed home from work and took aspirin. Harvey went off to work. When he got home, after riding PATCO, from his office in Philadelphia, Isolde said she hadn't slept, had had chills and muscle pain and was exhausted. Her temp had come down to 100 (37.8 C).

Harvey drove her to their primary care doctor. Harvey liked him. He was humorous. When Harvey had a small growth on the top of his head that needed to be removed, he asked this doctor, "It's a small operation, isn't it?"

The doctor laughed, "The definition of a small operation is something they do to someone else."

It took Harvey a few seconds to be sure it was a joke. He wasn't sure he approved of doctors telling jokes, but he immediately relaxed.

The doctor was concerned about the fever and prescribed various treatments. The temperature came down but was still above Isolde's normal temperature. She had chills, and then sweats, and muscle pain for five more days. Isolde's temperature finally returned to normal, but she didn't. She was exhausted, her muscles ached, and she felt depressed. Getting out of bed was an agony. "We'll get through this," she said to Harvey. He nodded, smiled and secretly worried.

For the next several weeks, Isolde saw specialists recommended by their doctor. They did extensive tests but didn't find anything wrong. The only time Isolde left the house was to visit doctors.

@@@@@@ MALINGERER @@@@@@

After three weeks, Isolde would have to either return to work, go on long-term disability, or quit her job. After much urging, their doctor reluctantly sent the company a note asking for a month of disability for Isolde. The month was spent having more tests. They found nothing.

A week later, Harvey returned from work to find Isolde in bed crying. When he asked what was wrong, Isolde said, "I'll never forgive that bastard. I've been turned down for additional disability."

"Show it to me," Harvey said. "It can't be all that bad. You know how difficult insurance companies can be."

Isolde handed Harvey the three-sentence letter which began, "Please excuse Isolde from work. She is malingering and cannot return to work at this time."

"Malingering?" Isolde shouted. She lay her head down and cried bitter tears. "Do you have any idea how many times I've tried to get up and go to work? I love work. I'd never malinger. I can't believe it. What are we going to do?"

"Malingering. I've never heard of a doctor saying that," replied Harvey. Isolde noticed the deep scowl on his face. "Just because he doesn't know what's wrong doesn't mean you're not sick. It's his fault not ours." Harvey didn't add, *and it's our problem.* Isolde was forced to resign her job.

Thousands of people across the world suffered from similar problems. It was given several names, multiple syndromes of vague symptoms. Several patient's organizations were founded to give encouragement, but no definite cause or cures were in the offing.

@@@@@@ IN YOUR HEAD @@@@@@

At least four or five times in the next year, Isolde would toss an article at Harvey. "Look at this. Another one," yelled Isolde. "Some stupid scientist determined it's all in my head. Clouded emotions and complexes. What the hell do they know about constantly being sick and tired, about despair? They're healthy."

Harvey tried to think of something to say that might help. Isolde's face got redder and her voice more ragged as she yelled, "You probably think I'm making this up too."

"No, never," Harvey said. He wanted to say more but he couldn't think of anything that might help. *We're both checkmated*, he thought.

@@@@@@ TEETH @@@@@@

"My problem might be related to having too much mercury and other heavy metals my blood." Isolde showed an article to Harvey. "It says taking the amalgam fillings out of your teeth and then having chelation therapy will take the excess metals out of your body. It might take a year or more after you do this to notice the improvement but we've got to try it."

Harvey heard himself ask out loud, "Have there been any peer-reviewed scientific studies that show this will cure your syndrome?" He saw Isolde flinch.

"It's too new. It hasn't been studied yet, but they say it often works." This conversation didn't convince Harvey but when you're chasing hope, it always appears about twenty steps in front of you, often fading away and then re-appearing again, always just beyond your grasp.

They started with their current dentist. After reading the article, the dentist asked, "Is it ethical? There's no evidence provided. You have fourteen fillings. Replacing them all could be dangerous to your health. I won't do it without a real study."

While driving home, Harvey said, "Maybe you could get a bunch of different dentists to do one or two fillings at a time."

"That would be too exhausting, and I couldn't lie to them."

Eventually, they found a dentist who agreed to do the work during four visits, one for each quadrant, each a week apart. They checked his disciplinary record, and he had one complaint filed against him.

"They don't put people on the list over a misunderstanding," said Harvey.

"One complaint? That's nothing. If he was a bad dentist, he'd have scores of them. He's brave and is willing to try new things. That's what counts."

Over a four-week period, all fourteen filings were removed. A few months later, Isolde didn't feel any different. They watched the beginning of the *Wide World of Sports* with the announcer calling out, "The thrill of victory and the agony of defeat."

"What if you never won or lost?" asked Isolde. "That's so much worse."

"Yes," agreed Harvey.

@@@@@@ DOCTOR OM @@@@@@

The spiritual healer, whom Harvey always thought of as "Doctor Om" popped into his thoughts. *What was his real name? I can't remember.* A fellow sufferer had recommended him to Isolde saying that he really helped her.

Doctor Om said on the phone that he understood how frustrated Isolde was with all the medical advice and treatments she'd had so far. "Science doesn't know everything. You need a wholistic approach to solve your health problems. Let ancient wisdom cure you." He said that he'd found that alternative, more spiritual means were the key to recovery for a patient with a disease not responding to so called scientific treatments. He offered such a service, which had helped many people. Harvey and Isolde reviewed the testimonials given by his patients and wanted to try it. He had an office two blocks away from Princeton University. It was an hour drive, but Isolde wanted to try it.

They arrived at his office at 7 p.m. He greeted them alone. He had no assistants, no nurses, no one to check them in. They wrote him a personal check for $500. He asked Isolde to come into his private sitting room.

"Can I be there?" asked Harvey.

"No. It works best with the patient and the healer only."

Harvey sat in the waiting room. A slight odor of frangipani incense came from under the door; along with a sound that reminded Harvey of the flutter of wings he'd heard beating in a butterfly pavilion. Fifteen minutes later, they came out. The doctor said, "You should start to see the effects in a few days. Keep a positive attitude."

When they got in the car and started driving, Isolde began fuming. "Do you know what he did?"

"No idea."

"He had me sit in a chair and close my eyes." Harvey was hoping they wouldn't have to contact the police. In his peripheral vision Harvey noticed Isolde turn her head to look directly at him. She waited and then continued. "He put his hands on my head and began to chant "OM" for the whole fifteen minutes.

"Nothing else?"

"Absolutely nothing." Harvey wondered if he should ask if she felt any better? He glanced over and saw her frown lit by road light. He thought that phrase would make a great song title. He didn't ask.

When they got home, Isolde spoke again. "He could have at least put some emotional energy into it. At one point I thought he'd fallen asleep. You could have chanted 'om' better." She paused for quite a while and then continued, "His dog gave me more emotional support than he did. He curled around my leg wagging his tail. I could tell he wanted me to be cured but I wasn't so sure about the healer."

"Should we report him to someone?"

"To whom? Should I stand in front of his office and warn his patients that he's a fraud? I don't have the energy for that. I should have asked way more questions before I went, and I didn't. I just feel stupid."

"So do I." Harvey didn't continue. He was remembering how stupid and dismayed he'd felt when he'd seen a notice for a Catholic healing service that featured the laying on of hands. He was Catholic. Isolde wasn't. He suggested they go. When the priest said that he was only allowed to pray over Catholics, Isolde whispered her anger, "I should write a letter of complaint to the Pope." Harvey thought, *the priest shouldn't have even asked her religion. He could have put his hands on her forehead and prayed. That couldn't hurt anyone. Maybe it would have helped in more ways than one.*

These two incidents, close together, formed the basis of an agreement they came to. At breakfast one Saturday, Isolde said, "God could cure me if He wanted to."

"What do you mean?" Harvey asked.

"I'll pray but I won't pay or beg for that kind of aid from any person."

"I agree."

@@@@@@ SUGGESTIONS @@@@@@

"I can't believe how everyone constantly keeps asking how I am," said Isolde one evening when Harvey came home from work.

"I'm sure they're just concerned with your health and are showing their love."

"Some of them are enjoying it. I can hear the joy in their voice when they talk to me."

"It's so hard to judge."

"And the suggestions?" continued Isolde, having ignored what Harvey had said. "Have you tried this? You should try that. They say, 'my friend has a similar problem and was cured by this BS treatment.' The suggestions are endless. I want to scream, I'm doing all I can."

"It's hard to understand when it doesn't happen to you."

"And we're barely making it. My mother keeps suggesting we move into their basement. I don't want to move back home."

"I found a part-time job delivering pizza at night. It will help keep us going."

"You're already working too hard. The only time I see you is at night."

"It's just for a while. You'll get better soon."

"How do you know?"

"I just do. Why there's …"

"Don't you dare make another treatment suggestion."

@@@@@@ THE EXPERT @@@@@@

"I finally got an appointment," said Isolde. "He's a renowned expert and researcher."

A week later, they were sitting in the expert's waiting room, in an expensive neighborhood in Philadelphia. The waiting room had about twelve chairs. There was a TV, the volume turned down low, showing CNN news.

A patient came out of the doctor's office and talked to the nurse, who gave her the bill.

"It lists an extra fifty for a B-12 shot and an additional twenty-five dollars to give the shot. I was told it costs two hundred fifty for a visit and everything would be included."

"We never told you that."

The woman began to cry. "I don't have insurance. I've a four-year-old daughter and I can't afford the extra money."

"We're very sorry."

"Sorry enough to drop the charges at least on the injection?"

"We can't do that."

Twenty-five to give a shot? Shouldn't that be part of the cost of the shot? B-12 can't cost that much, thought Harvey. He didn't say anything.

Isolde was with the doctor for a long time. He gave her a B-12 shot and a prescription for extensive blood tests, which might illuminate the obscure situation and aid his research.

On the way home Isolde was encouraged. The expert had some new ideas to try.

Two weeks later, Isolde saw the expert, who told her, that one of the blood tests showed she has a very common virus, which almost everyone has but for which there's no current treatment. Her immune system might have been weakened so she couldn't fight it. He gave her another B-12 shot. He asked her to get a second set of blood work done.

Two days later, when Harvey came home, Isolde was crying. She handed Harvey the insurance company's bill for the first blood work. It listed a comprehensive column of tests that together costs $7,347. The insurance company would cover $647, which they said was the reasonable and customary cost.

"Reasonable and customary is a scam," said Isolde. "How will we ever pay that much? And they've already done a second test we'll have to pay for."

"We'll manage somehow."

"We're the ones paying for his research."

Over the next two months, Isolde got eight more B-12 shots but refused to have any more of the expensive blood tests. There wasn't a noticeable improvement but each time she saw the expert she felt that maybe progress was being made towards a cure.

The expert kept dogging the insurance company to pay more of the blood tests fee. After three months, they agreed to pay almost all of it.

A year later, when Isolde applied for Social Security Disability, she was told to expect to be rejected and to have to appeal and go to trial. The government rejected most claims like hers. The expert provided extensive documentation of her condition, and, to their surprise, she was approved. She still didn't feel any better, but the extra income eased some of the financial burdens.

@@@@@@ INJECT GAS? @@@@@@

"We inject the gas directly into the blood," said the doctor. "It kills all viruses."

"Has there been any verified studies?" Harvey asked.

"We have had a great deal of success. I can't guarantee it will cure but it has been very helpful."

"I read that it might be corrosive," said Harvey. "The concentrations that would be needed to kill all the viruses might be dangerous."

"It's only money that keeps us from being approved," said the doctor. "The pharmaceutical industry isn't interested in cures. There's more money in treatments that don't work."

"I want to try it," said Isolde.

The doctor was four hundred miles away, near a high-school friend of Isolde, who had moved to Erie, Pennsylvania. She stayed there for five weeks, receiving treatment every second day. Harvey came up twice to visit.

During the stay, the doctor said that the FDA had decided to halt this therapy in the USA to do more study. "We're moving our therapy out of the country. It's going to take us at least eight months to get set up but I can give you the phone number of another doctor in Antigua who has amazing results."

@@@@@@ THE DRUG @@@@@@

"Yes, that makes sense," Harvey heard himself say on the call. He realized he'd been daydreaming and after another ten seconds, he was doing it again.

The key in the car's lock began to bend. *I'd better try another door*, thought Harvey. It was forty below (-40 C) and the locks had frozen. He'd stayed overnight near Brantford, Ontario waiting to visit the clinic where a preliminary study of an experimental drug was taking place. There was little data on its effectiveness, and it was illegal to import the drug into the USA.

Creak. Harvey was able to open the door on the passenger's side. He slid across the seat, which felt like it was made of steel and turned the key. Nothing. Cars don't start at forty below. He went back into the motel; they called to get him a boost.

An hour later, cash changed hands for eight vials of the precious drug. He'd gotten the expert to fill in an American prescription form. "It's not legal or proven," he said, "but it might help. If you get questioned, show them this prescription. There's a chance the border agent won't know it's not legal to import."

Harvey put the drugs and the prescription slip into the glove compartment and drove back to the States. At the border there were two cars in front of him. *How does one appear nonchalant?* he wondered.

"What was the purpose of your visit?" asked the agent.

"Sightseeing."

"How long have you been in Canada?" Harvey considered lying but he thought the agent could easily check to see how long he'd been there.

"One day."

"Where did you stay?"

"Brantford."

"That's no tourist destination. Can't do much sightseeing in one day when it's this cold." The agent frowned. "Pop the trunk." Harvey's heart raced. They never checked when he'd crossed the border with Isolde. He heard the agent unzip his suitcase.

When the agent said, "Drive on," Harvey drove off at the speed limit. A few minutes later, when the crossing was out of sight and there were no other cars nearby, Harvey pumped his fist and yelled, "I did it. My first smuggling operation."

@@@@@@ DO YOU LOVE YOUR WIFE? @@@@@@

"Are you listening?" Harvey heard from the phone. He realized he'd been daydreaming again. He lied, "Sorry.

I had a pot on the oven and had to turn it off. I missed about the last three minutes."

"I was explaining how I can cure any disease in three weeks."

"Any disease," Harvey said.

"Yes. Most of the people I cure had cancer. I personally guarantee I can cure your wife."

"How much is it again?"

"It's $3,000 per day. As I said, we just lowered the price."

"You're in Antigua? That means your treatment hasn't been checked out by the FDA?"

"If it's the money you're worried about, a cure is the most cost-effective treatment ever."

"I just don't know."

"If you love your wife, you'll do it. No question about it."

Harvey wanted to scream: *You ass. Of course I love my wife.* He continued listening and then hung up saying he'd speak to Isolde about it.

Later that day, Isolde asked whom Harry had been talking to. He wasn't sure he should answer. Maybe she'd think he was just being cheap. He told her about the call.

"You'd do it if you loved me?" asked Isolde. "He really said that?"

"Yup."

"That's emotional blackmail and fraud. No one can guarantee a cure. Let's make a deal, never to give in to anyone like that."

"I agree."

"Tests show my mercury level is now down to normal which is helping and with that Canadian drug I'm feeling a bit less fatigued. I walked around the block twice today. First time in years. Maybe you could drive up and get some more of that Canadian drug. That is if you love me," she smiled.

Harvey's eyes widened. He hesitated, smiled and hugged Isolde. He was about to joke "maybe," but he found himself saying, "Yes. This time I'll spend at least two days up there. Maybe spend a night on the Canadian side of Niagara Falls. Might look like I'm actually sightseeing. Something's bound to happen. You'll get better or I'll get arrested."

"If you love me," she laughed, and turned and walked towards the bedroom with a teeny spring in her step.

A walk around the block is no cure but to gain even a step on that elusive hope you've been chasing is exhilarating, almost like experiencing your first kiss. Harvey pumped his fist as joy and relief surged through his heart. Hope. There's nothing better than hope.

WHAT ARE YOU GOING TO DO WITH YOUR LIFE?

"What are you going to do with your life?" my mom asks quietly, her unsmiling stare drills into my eyes.

"I don't know Mom. I haven't even woken up yet."

"I know that" she says, a little louder. "It's a great time to think about what you intend to do with your life."

It's around 6:45 a.m. and we're in our kitchen before I walk to school. This question is repeated almost every school morning. It started when I was about nine. In winter, it is completely dark outside, a small wall lamp gives off a ring of light. In summer, bright sunlight jabs my eyes. Neither darkness nor light changes the question or gives me any idea of how I should answer. I drink some milk and eat my bagel quickly. I'm a bit late to start out.

Secretly, I call this performance, "My Interrogation" or "One More Impossible Question." Why is she asking? Is it a real question or a plea of some kind? Why doesn't she ask my brother or sister the same question? Is it because she sees more potential in me or maybe much less. Maybe it's my odd, and to her infuriating, insistence in agreeing with the different sides of every argument?

"How can something be true and not true at the same time?" she asks.

"I can't explain it, but I see two competing good ideas. They're both true."

"They can't both be true. You'll have to decide sometime," she says. "What ARE you going to do with your life?"

I want to shout, "I have no idea. Stop torturing me," but over the years I start to make up answers. "I'm going to be a firefighter." "I'm going to be a mathematical genius and prove the Goldbach conjecture." It doesn't matter that neither my mom nor I know what the Goldbach conjecture is.

She smiles. I think that answering the question might stop the questioning. I get a few days off, but inevitably, the question returns, with even more passion.

By the time I am a senior in high school, I want to ask my mom, "What gives you the right to ask me this question? What have you done?" I don't. I feel her love and concern and anguish. "What am I going to do with my life?" I ask myself. I have no idea.

A year later, she is diagnosed with cancer and has chemo, which suppresses the creation of platelets in the blood. She must receive donated platelets, so she won't bleed to death. They save her life for a time, but she dies two years later from the cancer, right before her first grandchild is born.

I am an unmarried, college dropout who works odd jobs. That early morning question still tortures me. It is also her gift which teaches that life is short. I should use it well before time evaporates. But what is a choice which will please her? What is a choice that will please me? I do not know.

Every few weeks I donate platelets. It takes two or more hours with a needle in your arm, and I hate doing it. The attendant says, "Good, the blood is flowing now." I don't look. The machine will take care of it without me looking. After an hour, I want it to be over. I take out a photo of my mom, holding me as a child, and say, "Mom, this is for you. Maybe someone will get a chance to hold their first grandchild. I wish you had that chance." And there's a feeling of warmth and even, on rare occasions, a feeling that I am doing something with my life.

THE GREAT SILENCE

I mustn't tell anyone. This warning, pounded gently but persistently in Doris' mind. She and her two children, Andrew, ten, and Maya, eight, were paddling not far from shore. Doris had rented a vacation cottage on Malletts Bay on Lake Champlain. It was 5 p.m., in mid-August. There was bright sunshine and a slight breeze creating maybe four-inch swells. The temperature was in the high-seventies. It was their first vacation since her husband's nuclear submarine tour began four months ago. He'd be gone for another two months.

Doris' thoughts continued as she watched Andrew and Maya race their kayaks towards the opposite shore. Maybe she should chase after them, in her rowboat, but she didn't. Normally, she'd be worried, but she wasn't now. Don't tell them, her mind continued. It wouldn't be fair to them. They wouldn't believe it anyway. They'll get jealous. I don't even know if I believe it.

Doris had a whistle they used to communicate while on the water. When she blew it, Andrew and Maya were supposed to turn around and come back to her. She blew and she saw the two of them slow down. About a minute later, she blew again, and they turned around and slowly paddled back towards her. They wanted to prolong this paddle as long as possible. It would take over ten minutes for them to get to her at their current rate. She could just enjoy what she was experiencing.

Doris put the oars down in the middle of the rowboat, leaned back, and just felt. What would she say if she decided to tell them and how would she explain how it had occurred. She began to think but then said out loud, "I'll just say it. No one can hear me here, except perhaps you Lord and you probably have better things to do than to listen to me at the current moment." She began to sing "Amazing Grace How Sweet the Sound That Saved a Wretch Like Me" but she felt, no I'm not a quite a wretch. Been confused for a long time. Exactly what am I feeling?

Joy, like a parched tongue with its first taste of a nectar sweeter than strawberry jam, she thought. No. It felt better than that. A person standing in the afternoon rain, where each raindrop was a warm drop of joy. No. There were no drops, only ecstasy. Maybe as if each red blood cell in her body were alive with continental sized delight. No. It was better than that. Her breathing slowed. It was like breathing in the essence of excited, calm, screamingly silent pleasure. Well not quite pleasure. Something more. Doris decided to give up trying to describe it. She wondered if she was in a manic stage, but she had never once had any symptoms of manic depression or manic euphoria. If she couldn't describe what she felt, no one else would even remotely believe her.

She began to wonder how did it start? She was both a believer and someone who did mental exercises. She didn't call them spiritual exercises, more like training exercises. Before the trip, she'd started another one. It was a simple question, which she had read and tried to give an honest answer to. She had a slip of paper in her pocket with the question. She took it out and read the question again. "What keeps me from dropping worry right now. Nothing."

Nothing. That word had vibrated in her mind when she read it. Strange to say but her mind now was completely silent. She might label her state as "The Great Silence" if she had any thoughts but there was no thought using words in this silence. There was just feeling and a clear knowledge of what she should do without any thinking using words.

She recalled the ride up to the lake. Just before Rutland, Vermont, their front left tire punctured. The car violently pulled left towards the fast lane. Unusually for her, she felt extremely calm as she coolly turned the steering wheel to the right and applied the brakes. There was about a six-foot wide pull-off lane with a drop of several feet on it's right. They ended up with the right front tire over the edge, balanced on three wheels.

Andrew had called out, "That was fun mom. Let's do it again."

Doris turned around and Maya was shivering in the back.

Doris reached back, put her hand on her shoulder and said, "It will be alright. Don't worry." She had her children step out of the car, go about fifty paces ahead. She waited until she couldn't see any cars coming and put the car in reverse, stepped on the gas hard and then slammed on the break. All four wheels were on the pavement.

"Let me do it next time," called out Andrew.

Maya looked at her mom in wonder. This wasn't the Doris she knew. She whispered to Andrew, "What's going on? Mom's so calm."

Andrew answered loudly, "Just like I'd be."

Doris emptied the trunk and got out the full-sized spare tire and the jack. Andrew helped her change the tire and then they were off.

They'd stopped at Price Chopper to pick up food. They got to their rented, small, two-bedroom cottage that sat about fifty feet from the lakeshore, around 4 p.m. There was a fire pit with a huge pile of split logs next to it, two kayaks and a rowboat turned over and a grill in the yard. There was a twenty-foot dock and an offshore swimming platform about fifty or sixty yards from shore. They settled their luggage and went for a paddle.

By this time the children had made it back to her. They got back to the shore, turned their watercrafts over, and went inside. The children began to play video games while Doris made their favorite supper of macaroni and cheese. Price Chopper had guacamole, which was also a favorite. They'd have it with chips. Cooking did not distract from what she was feeling. Rivers of bliss are falling on my head, she felt. No that's just a cliché. What does it really feel like? It was almost overwhelming. A meteor falling into the atmosphere, creating a bright line of light of exaltation but the meteor kept getting bigger and the light kept getting stronger and the meteor wasn't falling but just gliding, getting bigger and bigger, brighter and brighter but there was absolutely nothing to worry about. Why would she be worrying?

Dinner passed pleasantly. They watched the sun go down across the lake. Andrew reminded her that she'd promised to let them build a fire in the fire pit and make s'mores. Before they went out, she put some bug spray on her kids but forgot to put it on herself.

Andrew quickly arranged split logs to make a large fire over some newspaper kindling. He lit it and watched the wood catch fire.

"This is great wood," he declared as the fire rapidly grew.

Doris knew Andrew would continue to add logs until she stopped him, or the fire was so big that he would yell,

"The fire is taller than my head." He was a lot like his dad, always ready for an adventure.

Andrew was shocked that his mom hadn't told him to stop so he added three more logs. What was going on with her? The flames leapt a little higher than his head. He picked up another two logs, looked over to Maya who shook her head, no, indicating that the fire was already too large. Doris said nothing. He added them. There was still no response from Doris. By this time, even Andrew was a bit overawed by the size of the fire and he decided not to add yet another log.

The three stared into the fire. Each in their own worlds. Maya was missing her father. Why was he away so much? Couldn't he find another job so he could stay with them? She looked over at Doris who was shooing some mosquitos away. It was about the sixth bite she'd noticed. Most were around her ankles or hands. She started to scratch.

"Been bitten mom?" asked Andrew.

"Sure have."

"I haven't heard you complain," said Maya.

"I'm not complaining anymore."

"You always complain about mosquito bites," said Andrew.

Maya said, "You always ask why God created mosquitos? You said it's the only mistake He ever made."

"God doesn't make mistakes," said Doris.

"So it doesn't bother you?" asked Andrew.

"Nothing bothers me tonight."

"Nothing?" asked Maya.

"What if I caught fire?" asked Andrew.

"I'd drag you to the lake and put it out."

"And you wouldn't be worried?" asked Andrew.

"Worry would be the wrong word," said Doris.

"I don't understand," said Maya.

"I don't understand either," said Doris. "Everything is just so wonderful. So perfect." As soon as she said this there was the faintest feeling that she'd said too much. She'd promised herself to say nothing about what she was feeling.

"Daddy's not here," said Maya. "That's not perfect."

"I wish he were here too," said Doris.

"But everything's perfect?" asked Maya.

"Well yes." Doris couldn't think of anything else to say that they'd understand or that would be helpful. She felt she was breathing ever-new joy. "I'm going to get what we need to make s'mores." She went into the house.

"What's gotten into mom?" asked Maya.

"I don't know," said Andrew. "She should have stopped me from putting on that last log."

"She should have been upset about the bites," said Maya. "She says the world is perfect. Who is she kidding? It's horrible. There's climate change and poor people and …"

Andrew interrupted, "Plus, the Yankees are doing terrible this year."

"Only idiots care about that," said Maya. "What's worse is that mom doesn't care about us."

"Maybe we should test her. See if she can stay happy when we make her life miserable."

"That would be mean," said Maya.

"No, it wouldn't. We'll just keep it up until she admits there's rotten things happening."

"I not sure," said Maya.

"It will be fun. Let's do it."

Maya sat and thought. "I'll go this far. Let's ruin the s'mores and see how mom reacts. We'll stop after that."

"Yeah," said Andrew. "That's a plan. We'll just see what happens and then we can stop."

"It's a deal." Both were smiling.

Doris came out with a tray containing graham crackers, marshmallows, chocolate bars, and long sticks to roast the marshmallows on.

"Let's roast a few marshmallows by themselves first," said Andrew. Maya immediately knew his plans. Whereas she and Andrew liked to burn their marshmallows and eat them, Doris always slowly roasted hers to a golden brown and then ate it. He was going to make sure her marshmallow caught on fire.

Usually, Maya and Andrew would have their marshmallows in the fire long before Doris started. This time they waited. When Doris held hers away from the flames but close enough to brown, Andrew put a marshmallow on his stick and used it to poke Doris' stick into the fire. Doris' marshmallow caught fire, and she laughed. "It will be a new experience," she said. "Who says marshmallows don't taste good burned." She blew the flame out and ate it.

"Delicious," she said. Maya and Andrew looked at each other in disbelief. This obviously was going to be much harder than they'd thought. A conspiratorial smile passed between them. Doris, who was enjoying the taste, didn't notice.

Doris took a second marshmallow and started toasting it. Maya and Andrew ate their burnt ones and burnt a second set.

"Time to make s'mores," said Doris.

"I'll get the graham crackers and chocolate," said Andrew. He's being unusually cooperative tonight, thought Doris. He picked up the tray, carried it towards the fire, intentionally tripped and the contents flew into the fire. He'd fallen several feet from the fire and was completely safe.

"I tripped," he called out.

"You're always tripping," said Maya.

"No, I'm not," said Andrew. "You're the one who trips."

"Well, no s'mores but we still have some marshmallows," said Doris. A fire of delight warmed her heart. The three contentedly ate some more marshmallows. The moon rose casting shimmering lights on the lake. "What a glorious night," Doris said. Maya and Andrew sat silently.

The next morning, at breakfast, Andrew poured salt in Doris' coffee when she wasn't looking. When she tasted it, she threw the coffee in the sink and made herself another cup without saying a word.

It was a warm sunny morning. "Can we go swimming," asked Andrew.

"You have to wait an hour before you go in?"

"I want to go now," said Maya.

"You could get cramps," said Doris in as stern tone as she could muster. To her surprise her children agreed. They'd sit on the dock until it was swimming time. They put on their bathing suits, some suntan lotion, and went to sit on the dock, kicking the water and doing a bit of splashing with each other.

"We've got to really up our game," said Andrew.

"Haven't we done enough already?" asked Maya. A few seconds later she asked, "What do you have in mind?"

"Are you definitely in?"

"I'm not sure," said Maya.

"Well then you'll just have to wait and see."

Fifty minutes later Doris came out in her bathing suit. All three were good swimmers. The water didn't get deep quickly and by the time Maya had to swim because the water was over her head, they were only about fifteen yards from the swimming platform. In another three yards, Andrew had to start swimming. When they got to the platform, Maya climbed on, but Andrew kept swimming. That wasn't so unusual. Doris expected that he'd soon turn around and come back but he kept going further and further from shore.

In joy she watched him. No thoughts crossed her mind. She was in The Great Silence. When he got about a hundred and fifty yards past the platform, without thought Doris started to swim slowly in his direction. She wished she'd taken the whistle, but she hadn't. It's really strange, she thought. The joy's even stronger.

She heard Maya call out over and over, "Come back Andrew." Andrew kept swimming further from shore. He was a faster swimmer than Doris. She wasn't sure what would happen if he got into trouble. She probably couldn't pull him to shore. She swam back to the shore. She put on her life preserver and took an extra one for Andrew. The rowboat had a rope that he could hold on to if she needed to pull him back to shore. She got in and started to row towards Andrew.

She looked over at Maya, who was crying on the platform. "Don't you dare leave that platform," she cried out. By this time, Andrew was almost a quarter of a mile out and still swimming away. She rowed as fast as she could and in about eight minutes was within ten yards of him.

Her mind was still silent. She called out, "Andrew, it's time to turn around and come back." She waited for his response.

He turned his head towards her. It might have been the first time he realized just how far out he was. It looked to her as if he was panicking. His head slid below the water. He flailed his hands in the air. She took the extra life preserver, jumped out, swam to Andrew and pulled him up.

He floated onto his back and said, "Fooled you mom." Her hand grabbed his shoulder and shook it. She yelled, "Don't ever fool around in deep water."

He put on to the life preserver. They slowly swam their way back to the swimming platform where Maya was still crying. All three swam to shore.

"Don't ever do that again," Maya yelled at Andrew. "You scared the hell out of me."

To Doris' amazement, the joy kept coming. She heard herself say, "Maybe we'd better just go home."

"No, mom," said Andrew. "We're having a great vacation."

"I don't want to go either," said Maya.

"Are you two going to behave?" asked Doris.

"I didn't do anything wrong," said Andrew. "I was just fooling around."

"Maybe we should stay inside for the day," said Doris. The children went into the cottage while Doris took a kayak, paddled to the rowboat, and towed it to shore.

At lunch, Maya said, "You promised to take us to Ethan Allen's house. We're studying him in the fall."

Around 2 p.m., they drove to Ethan Allen's homestead. During the tour, the guide said that Ethan had gone to visit some friends when he was fifty and, on the way back, he collapsed and died the next day.

"Did he say anything after he collapsed?" asked Andrew.

"No. He never said another word."

On the way home, they stopped at the Price Chopper. Doris bought some fresh corn. They'd have that and hamburgers cooked on the grill. As she was cooking the hamburgers she prayed that the joy would leave her. "It isn't helping anyone," she said out loud.

There was no answer. The next morning, she woke up and was still in The Great Silence. Andrew did not put salt in her coffee. She wondered how long this joyous silence would continue. I'm not going to worry about it was her only thought.

Writer's Heaven

"I can't tell you how much it means to me to be here in Writer's Heaven." says Jessica Hurling, the author of three best-selling novels including *Love's Glory Days*.

"We deserve it", says Ernest Hemingway, who has a scotch in one hand and is smoking a Cuban cigar. "I'm so glad they haven't forgotten me."

"I never expected a heaven for writers in the first place," says Norman Mailer. "By the way, how did you get here Hemingway? Suicides are supposed to go to hell. Sylvia Plath isn't here."

The three were sitting in a theatre seating about four hundred, looking at a monitor that covers the entire stage. There were hundreds of similar theatres in Writer's Heaven.

"Cut the crap about my suicide," answers Hemingway. "Always taunting me and everyone else. I got so damned depressed. There seemed no other way out."

"I understand completely, Ernest," says Hurling. "What's important is that you're here. I'm nervous about this week's results. They'll be posted in about a minute."

"You're not quite as high on the board as you used to be," says Mailer as he looks at Hemingway.

"It's being on the board long term that counts, not the weekly ups and downs," says Hemingway. "My books and the movies based on them are viewed thousands of times a day plus I get hundreds of articles written about me every year. That's why all five of my current popularity indicators on the status board are blue, which is an even higher rating than green. You've starting to get mostly yellow indicators, Mailer, and only one green one."

"That's nothing compared to the hurt they're putting on Hurling," says Mailer. "Down to only one yellow indicator and all the rest reds."

"I'm sure I'll do better this week," says Hurling.

"I've always been jealous of Agatha Christie," says Mailer. "Her works are read far more than any of ours."

"Where is she?" Asks Hurling. "I haven't seen her in years."

"We don't have to be in a theatre when the new weekly statuses are revealed," says Hemingway. "Christie's probably watching remote."

"I feel sorry for those who slip down to no interest," says Mailer. He looks over at Hurling, who is red with jealousy. "They're forced to leave Writer's Heaven."

"You call yourself my friend," says Hurling, "and all you do is insult me because I'm falling in the standings."

"You knew back then that best sellers like yours didn't have staying power," says Mailer. "Did you really think you'd be here forever?"

"You forget," says Hurling, "that three weeks ago, there was a major article about me."

"Yeah, under a headline about forgotten authors," says Mailer. "It said your novels didn't age well."

"That article will push my numbers up. My books are really good."

The board flickers on with the headline, "Status Results for the Week of December 27." The results list the ratings of the writers in the room in descending contemporary popularity. Hemingway is near the top with five blue statuses. Mailer is in the middle with two greens, two yellow and one red. They must look all the way to the bottom of the list to see Hurling's standings.

"Bummer," says Hemingway to Hurling. "All red this week. I am truly sorry."

"They should give me another week," says Hurling. "I know my numbers will be better next week."

"You can't be surprised," says Mailer. "I'm certainly not."

An old man dressed in red comes up to Hurling and says, "It's time to leave. Come with me."

"I was hoping to stay. I'm not ready to go. Can I say goodbye to my friends?"

"Of course."

Hurling, Hemingway, and Mailer shake hands. "Goodbye friends," she says.

On the way out, Hurling asks the old man, "Can you answer a few questions for me?"

"I'll try my best."

"Why haven't I seen Agatha Christie in Writer's Heaven? She has a vast following."

"Writer's Heaven?" asks the old man. "You were never told that this is Writer's Heaven. How could it be heaven to sit around, gabbing about the past and waiting for a weekly reveal of how people, you have no contact with, think about you?"

"Are you saying that this is Writer's Hell?" asks Hurling.

"Writer's Hell? No one ever told you that either. You were told this is a Writer's Haven. That's an entirely different thing."

"What's the difference?"

"This is a haven for those writers who still obsess about their fame," says the old man. "Many can't deal with the finality of losing everything in death."

"But why isn't Christie here then?" asks Hurling. "Doesn't she care to be remembered?"

"She no longer cares so she was free to move on and she did."

"I don't understand. What's the purpose of this Writer's Haven?"

"Hopefully to get these stuck writers to forget the past and start to move on to new lives."

"How does a weekly board do that?" asks Hurling.

"In theory, writers like Hemingway and Mailer should conclude that they're reputation is solid, and they can stop monitoring it and just move on."

"But they haven't moved on," says Hurling.

"I said in theory."

"And no longer popular writers like me?"

"Will realize that no one any longer cares about their works, so there's no longer a reason to think about them," says the old man. "They'll realize that it's time to move on."

"And you think that taking me out of Writer's Haven is going to help me?" asks Hurling.

"We can only provide a way and place for you to change. To actually change is entirely up to you."

"Where are we going?" asks Hurling.

"That too is entirely up to you."

About the Author

Raymond Fortunato writes in Westchester, New York. He has a B.A. in history and mathematics and two master's degrees in history and English Literature. He's interested in humans, how they relate to themselves, to each other and to the worlds beyond themselves, both seen and unseen. His stories exploring what his characters think but do not always share with others or even know themselves. The stories are surprising because the author begins writing with no preconceived idea what the characters will choose, of their own accord and nature, to do. He is interested in and has studied many areas including but not limited to art, music, literature, history, writing, mathematics, physics, astrophysics, psychology, philosophy, religion, economics and politics. This broad range of interests, along with a very active imagination, allows him to write a wide variety of compelling stories.

Instagram @raymondfortunatoauthor
RaymondFortunato.com

Photo Credit: CanoeTheWild.com

9 798995 190806